Andy McBean
And the War of the Worlds

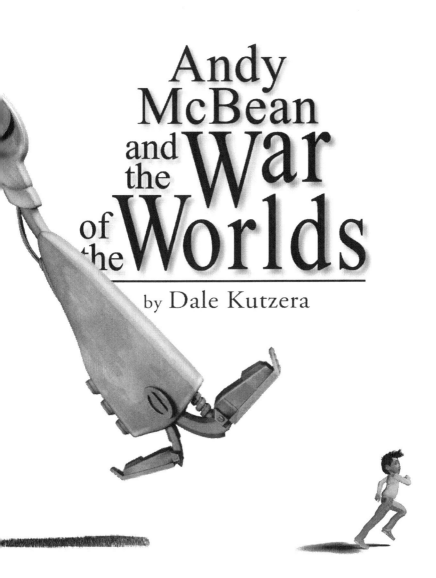

Andy McBean and the War of the Worlds

by Dale Kutzera

Salmon Bay Books

Contents

To H.G. Wells
For Invading my Imagination

This was no rock at all, but a machine made by an intelligence
very different from his own.

A Visitor From Another World

The tiny object burned white hot as it entered the Martian atmosphere. Black smoke trailed from its heat shield, drawing a straight line across the orange sky. High above the red landscape, parachutes unfurled, slowing the machine's descent as it soared over a canyon ten times wider than any found on Earth.

Having performed their brief task successfully, the chutes jettisoned and floated away. As the machine continued its descent, bulbous cushions burst around it like kernels of popcorn, softening its impact just north of the canyon rim. It slammed into the red soil, raising a cloud of dust, then leaped back into the air. Again and again it bounced across the rocky plane, kicking up orange plumes, each leap bringing it closer to a much larger machine that sat on the edge of the chasm like a temple to a very important god.

The larger machine, called a Vaporator, stood on three enormous feet, its hull encrusted with pipes and conduits. A dark opening dominated one side. Dust and the scant vapor in the planet's atmosphere swirled around the opening before being sucked inside.

Several tentacles, called Grabbers, pushed vast quantities of red soil onto a conveyor belt that led to the opening. The red planet looked dry, but its soil was filled with the frozen particles of moisture. The Vaporator would extract every bit of it, a task it had performed on numerous planets across the galaxy. So noisy and dusty was the water-mining operation that no one on the Vaporator noticed the small blob fall from the sky and bounce across the planet's surface. When the object finally collided into the Vaporator's hull, not even the operator of the Grabbers noticed.

His name was Been'Tok and he was small for his species, even for a Worker Drone. Brown fur covered his pear-shaped body from the top of his head to the wide toes on each of his three feet. His mouth was wide and shaped like an inverted-V. Just above it were three eyes; a large one for seeing far away things and two smaller ones for studying close-up things.

His only garment was the metal harness all Workers wore around their shoulders. The device filtered the air he breathed, recorded his work progress, stored information, and allowed the Masters to tell him he was working too slowly, or not carefully enough, or with an insufficiently positive attitude.

Been'Tok often had an insufficiently positive attitude. He found work boring and, far worse, a distraction from his hobby of collecting and studying growing things. He marveled at the immense canyon before him and focused all three of his eyes on the cliffs eroded long ago by torrents of water. It seemed impossible that so much liquid could have once covered the surface of this dusty orb, but the proof was all around him. He closed his eyes and imagined the river that had cut the chasm, the lakes and falls that fed it, and the lush banks of foliage that must have grown around them.

He grinned at the vision, but an alarm shattered his daydream. The metal plates beneath his feet shuddered to a halt. The flow of dirt on the conveyor stopped with a lurch. Been'Tok shut off the alarm and paused to appreciate the quiet breeze and the rhythmic clicking of his respirator.

He moved his hands through the Grabbers' holographic controls and directed one tentacle into the mound of dirt on the conveyor. It emerged a moment later clutching an unusual white stone. Been'Tok asked the Grabber to set it on a nearby exam table. The rock didn't look like much, just a craggy lump of volcanic basalt, but across one face grew a patch of white lichen that resembled a forest on very a tiny planet.

Been'Tok smiled, eager to study the plant life, but the projector on his harness glowed to life. A swarm of lights formed into the head of Master Tarak'Nor. The Masters were large, their heads as big as Been'Tok's entire body. Torak'Nor's face, streaked with gray, towered over him. The Master demanded to know the cause of the delay, and Been'Tok sheepishly revealed the strange stone. The Vaporator automatically shut down when it sensed living matter, but Tarak'Nor dismissed the rock without a moment's consideration. The lichen was an insignificant form of life and no reason to stop work.

Been'Tok grimaced as Tarak'Nor's image faded from view. The lichen would not be added to Been'Tok's collection of strange growing things. It would be vaporized and the drops of moisture it held added to the liquid the Vaporator was accumulating. There was a quota to be met and the sooner they reached it, the sooner they could leave this planet for the next one, and the next, and the next.

For a moment, Been'Tok considered keeping the stone for himself. He knew such disobedience would result in a visit by a Guardian. They were three times Been'Tok's height, twice his width, and their only task was to make sure Workers followed the Masters' orders. So with a sigh of resignation, Been'Tok placed the stone inside an evaporation chamber where it shook violently then burst into a reddish cloud that was quickly sucked away.

He returned to his station and, with a few gestures through the holographic controls, brought the conveyor back to life. The tentacles once again clawed at the red soil, resuming their dusty task. Been'Tok assumed the excitement for the day had passed when something else on the planet surface caught his attention.

This was no small rock, but a large boulder of shimmering white. He would take no chances with this discovery. Rather than ask a Grabber to bring the boulder to him, he would go to it. One tentacle gently wrapped itself around his body and carried him down the hull of the Vaporator to the dirt below. Once released, Been'Tok noted the puffy blobs had deflated, their white fabric draped over a hard square object. This was no rock at all, but a machine made by an intelligence very different from his own.

Two metal wings sprang open on the device revealing a small contraption perched on six wheels. Been'Tok backed away nervously. Even the Grabber seemed wary, ready to carry him to safety at a moment's notice.

A metal arm rose from the body, topped by two polished discs. They reminded Been'Tok of eyes and he wondered why there were only two. Stepping closer, he waved at the glass discs, unaware that fifty million kilometers away, on the third planet from the sun, a control room full of scientists gasped at the sight of him.

Andy McBean crept through the damp forest,
certain he was being followed.

CHAPTER ONE

Rainy Monday

A ndy McBean crept through the damp forest, certain he was being followed. Rain fell around him, dripping off fir trees, splatting over his red coat, and matting his black hair. It dribbled around his wide, gentle eyes, off his narrow cheeks and under the collar of his shirt, worming its way in cold trickles down his back. Andy hated the rain, and more fell in this soggy, mossy, drippy corner of the Pacific Northwest than almost anywhere else in the world.

The chorus of drips and splats could not mask the sound of footsteps behind him. At least he *thought* they were behind him. A moment ago the sound came from somewhere up the trail, but Andy couldn't trust his hearing. It hadn't been the same since his illness.

A year ago he could hear just fine, but the months he had spent in the hospital changed all that. When he emerged from the hospital after treatment, he was skinny and bald, his vision fuzzy, and hearing muffled. Over the past eight months, he had regained the weight, his eyesight had cleared, and his hair had grown back into a tangled mess, the front locks shooting out from his forehead like a hood ornament. His hearing, however, had never been the same.

He proceeded down the forest trail as quietly as possible, turning this way and that to better detect any sound. It was no small task given that he carried his trombone in one hand, his phone in the other, and a heavy backpack of books over his shoulders. He felt like a pack mule and ill-prepared to evade whatever it was that stalked him.

A twig snapped.

Andy froze, but saw nothing in the shadowy bushes. Something jumped from behind a tree, landing in the trail straight ahead. Andy's phone yelped, "Zoink!"

"Hah, gotcha!" Hector Moreno shouted. "That's three Zoinks. I win."

"No fair, Hector," Andy said. "You only have to carry a clarinet. I have to lug this trombone."

Hector pocketed his phone, the morning game of Zoink over. He was three months and five days older than Andy, two and three-quarter inches shorter, and twenty-three pounds heavier. In all the places Andy was skinny, Hector was round. Where Andy's eyes were blue, Hector's were brown. Where Andy was pale, Hector was tan even in the sunless months of winter. They were opposites in almost every respect, and best friends.

"You should have thought of that before joining the brass section, you dope."

"Dork."

"Spaz."

"Dweeb."

The boys continued down the drippy trail. They played Zoink almost every morning. The game was a kind of digital paint-ball where each boy shot at the other's phone, drenching the screen with gobs of colorful pixels. Each successful hit counted as a Splat, five Splats a Zoink, and three Zoinks a win.

The boys emerged from the forest where the trail ended at the back play field of Taggert Middle School. No longer shielded by the canopy of trees, they were pelted with rain from every direction. They trudged across the field through puddles large and small. Andy's arms ached from the weight of his trombone, but he knew the only thing worse than carrying a trombone was carrying a clarinet.

Everyone knew clarinets and flutes were for girls, a fact Hector was reminded of on a daily basis. Maybe that was why he was Andy's best and only friend. In the pecking order of Middle School, *the boy who played clarinet* fared no better than *the boy who had cancer*.

Hector studied the gloomy clouds. "Steady drizzle. I bet we have P. E. inside today."

"They'll call it a heavy mist and shove us outside whether we want to go or not."

"Maybe we can play soccer."

Andy stepped into a deeper than expected puddle and felt the water seep inside his shoe. "Nah, field is too mushy. They'll make us run laps."

"You gonna try out for the team this year?"

"I want to," Andy replied, "but I don't think my folks will let me. Man, I hate the rain."

"What'ya got against the rain, Andy? It's just water."

"Water in my face, running down my shirt, soaking my feet. Why couldn't I have been born in some hot place, where the sun shines and you wear T-shirts and shorts all year long?"

"Yeah. Blue sky. Heat," Hector nodded. "I lived in Arizona before moving here. It was killer-hot in the summer. And nothing grows there but cactus. I like the rain. More stuff grows here. Besides, it's stupid to get mad at something you can't do anything about."

"You calling me stupid?"

"If the shoe fits."

"Dork."

"Spaz."

"Dweeb."

"Barf-face."

"Barf-breath."

"That's a good one," Hector laughed. "I hate barf-breath. My mom makes me drink orange juice after I throw-up to get rid of the stink."

"Tell me about it."

Hector fell quiet. Andy had thrown-up a lot during his illness and that was the one subject neither boy talked about. It was an unspoken rule between them that the dark times in the hospital would never be discussed. Andy had enough reminders from his parents, neighbors, teachers, and fellow students who often whispered as he passed in the corridor, "*There goes cancer boy.*"

Hector changed the subject. "Maybe you're right. It is more of a heavy mist."

His voice trailed off as he stepped onto the running track. A quartet of dark figures beneath the bleachers grabbed his attention. They were dressed in black, from the dark boots on their feet to the black hoodies and beanies that covered their heads. The only color came from the red cinders of the cigarettes they smoked.

"Look straight ahead," Andy whispered. "Don't make any eye contact."

They walked on quickly, eyes straight ahead.

"Hey!" one of the silhouettes yelled.

Andy knew the voice. Reggie Grant was the leader of the small group of Goths that lurked under the bleachers or by the dumpsters outside the cafeteria. He and his friends, Ben Hickman and Lance Walker, all wore black and had the pocked faces and wispy mustaches of eighth graders. Even Lori Pitts, the only girl of the group, wore black save for the purple streaks in her hair.

"McBean!" Reggie yelled again. "Don't make me come get you."

Andy and Hector stopped mid-puddle and faced the misfit crew. The smell of sweat and tobacco fell over them as Reggie approached. Hector clutched his clarinet tight. Andy looked toward the science building a short distance away. Could they run to its safety before being caught? Probably not. Reggie had lousy endurance but was fast in short bursts.

"Look, it's cancer boy and clarinet girl," he said.

"You should start a legion of super-dorks," Lori added.

Ben Hickman licked his lips. "You got any food?"

"So cancer boy, when you croaked, did you see a light?"

"I didn't croak, Reggie. I was just sick," Andy replied.

"He came close," Hector added.

"Hector…"

"Well, you did."

"Can you see dead people now?" Lori asked.

"No… I was just sick."

"For like a year."

"Four months. And I'm better now. It's old news. Nothing to see here, folks. Move right along."

"Sandwiches? Cookies? Candy?" Ben asked again.

"You don't want to eat cancer boy's food," Reggie said. "He's radioactive. It might kill you."

The four Goths chuckled. They didn't notice the dark look in Andy's eyes or how his face flushed warm and red.

They completely missed how he gripped his trombone case so tight that his knuckles turned white. He was *cancer boy,* what could he possibly do?

Andy had endured a lot because of his illness and long treatment. He missed the entire soccer season and months of school. He spent the brief sunny weeks of summer confined, too weak to move, in a smelly hospital room. And he had been the target of countless looks of pity and concern. But the laughter of Reggie and his group of losers was just too much.

With a grunt, Andy rammed his trombone into Reggie's stomach. The older boy doubled over. Air woofed from his lungs. Ben, Lance, and Lori stopped laughing, shocked at the sight. No one hits their leader, let alone a sixth-grader who was a head shorter and thirty pounds lighter.

Even Andy was amazed at what his arms had done, but before he could recover his senses and dash to the science building, Reggie had lifted him off his feet and slammed him onto the muddy running track. The teenager's first punch caught Andy in the chest, but the second connected with his chin. Reggie's friends cheered him on while Hector stood frozen, mouth gaping and eyes wide.

Then someone shouted, "What is going on here!?"

It was Mrs. Russell, the girls' gym teacher. She marched toward them, her bright tracksuit shimmering in the misty rain. Mrs. Russell had the legs of a sprinter and the broad shoulders of a champion swimmer. With one hand, she grabbed Reggie and pulled him off Andy. With the other, she plucked the cigarette that still dangled from his lips and dropped it into a puddle.

Reggie turned bright red. The only thing worse than being rammed by cancer boy was being manhandled by the girls' Phys-Ed teacher.

"Reggie, principal's office," Mrs. Russell ordered.

"But I..."

"Go!"

Reggie glared at Andy and Hector. They all knew a line had been crossed. Reggie was not the sort of person you ram with a musical instrument. Ben, Lance, and Lori traded nervous glances then bolted toward the school. Finally, Reggie followed, staring daggers over his shoulder at Andy.

Mrs. Russell helped Andy to his feet and brushed some mud from his jacket, her eyes now soft with concern. "Are you all right?"

Andy was familiar with the look. He'd seen it all too often since being diagnosed. "I'm fine."

"You should go see the school nurse."

"I said I'm fine."

"Just to be safe," Mrs. Russell said. "I'll take you myself. Hector, get to class. The bell is about to ring."

Andy reached for his trombone, but Mrs. Russell picked it up for him. She took his arm and led him toward the school offices through the rain, which had, without a doubt, turned to a steady drizzle.

The day was off to a bad start; first losing at Zoink to Hector, then a fight with Reggie, and now the indignity of having Mrs. Russell carry his trombone for him. Andy was filled with gloom. He knew Mondays set the tone for the entire week.

CHAPTER TWO

A New Friend

The school nurse took Andy's temperature, checked his pulse and blood pressure, and asked him how he felt at least a dozen times. Andy was used to the routine. It happened every time he so much as appeared tired to one of his teachers.

The nurse was fully aware of his illness, the months he had spent in the hospital, and his delicate condition, which he insisted was neither delicate nor even a condition. He cooperated with her poking and prodding, vowing to return to the infirmary the instant he felt dizzy or light-headed.

In return, the nurse promised not to call his mother.

The only thing that made Andy dizzy or light-headed was the prospect that his mother would learn he had been in a fight. It would send her over the edge. She would check for cuts and bruises, send him to bed, then call Doctor Hilyard who would eventually calm her down, but not before Andy had spent another afternoon imprisoned in his bedroom.

And there were more immediate concerns, namely avoiding Reggie Grant. Andy went into stealth mode. He stayed clear of the main school building where Reggie had his locker. He took longer, less traveled paths from one class to the next. Skulking about, he thought of himself as a mouse darting between the feet of dinosaurs, but took some comfort in the knowledge that the dinosaurs had gone extinct while the furry mammals they terrorized had evolved to dominate the Earth as human beings.

During lunch, Andy sought refuge in the school library. He was fairly certain Reggie never visited the library and, quite possibly, didn't even know what a library was. Just in case, he sat at a table visible to the librarian, Mrs. Heinrich, whose stern presence discouraged any offense. There he tried to finish the Jack London short story assigned by Mr. Taylor, his English teacher.

"I thought I'd find you here."

Andy jumped. "Hector! Jeez Louise!"

"Sorry," Hector replied, pulling up a chair. "I haven't seen you all day."

"I'm in stealth mode."

"I hear that. Reggie got detention. He's gotta be pissed. What were you thinking, hitting him with your trombone like that?"

"I wasn't thinking. It just sort'a happened."

"Spaz."

"Dweeb."

"Doofus."

"Dope."

"Geek."

Mrs. Heinrich scowled from her desk. "Shhhhh."

The bell rang. Andy shoved his books into his backpack and the boys walked to the exit. Andy hadn't finished the short story *To Build a Fire*, but felt he could bluff his way through class. After all, he'd built plenty of fires camping in the forests around West Bend.

Hector studied his shoes. "I should have helped you. I thought about it. I was about to let loose with my banshee yell when Mrs. Russell showed up."

"Your banshee yell?" Andy asked.

"Yeah, it's killer. Terrifying. Like a dagger to the heart. Considered lethal in thirty-seven states."

Andy rolled his eyes. "Only thirty-seven? Last time it was forty-two."

"I'm serious."

"I am too. I have Reggie in art class."

"You can't go, Andy. You gotta skip."

"I never skip art. It's like the one class I really look forward to."

"If you go, he'll call you out," Hector warned. "He'll tell you to meet him at Founders Park so he can kick your butt. And if you refuse, he'll tell everyone you're chicken and your reputation will be ruined."

"I don't have a reputation."

"You might want one someday and this will kill your chances. Skip art class. Go back to the school nurse and tell her you puked or got the runs."

The boys exited the library and joined the flow of students in the corridor. Hector headed off toward Earth sciences and was soon lost in the crowd. Andy left the main building to take the less traveled route to English.

The knot in Andy's stomach only grew larger, though Mr. Taylor never called on him to discuss the Jack London story. There was a moment in social studies when he considered Hector's suggestion of visiting the school nurse. Didn't the nervous dread in his gut count as an illness?

Skipping art class, however, would mean losing a day's work on his painting. Andy had labored on a portrait of his dad for weeks. Martin McBean was an engineer and work had been slow over the past year. Andy hoped the painting would cheer him up. After all, no matter how difficult things were, his dad still took time to play catch with Andy and teach him the difference between a knight and a rook.

McBeans did not run from their responsibilities.

Andy went to art class and sat at his usual desk near the back lockers. He set out the portrait and gathered brushes, paints, and a jar of turpentine. There was no lecture in the class. The teacher simply paced the room offering words of encouragement and warning older students to keep the subject matter of their paintings clean. The door opened. Andy braced himself as Reggie entered.

The big eighth-grader stormed to Andy's desk, pushing aside anyone in his way. "McBean, you're toast!" he hissed. "You got me detention. They think I started the fight."

"You did start the fight."

"But you hit me first. Be at Founder's Park behind the ball field. Three o'clock. Don't make me find you."

To underscore his point, Reggie tipped over the jar of turpentine on Andy's desk. The liquid spilled over the portrait, causing the colors to streak and smear as though his dad's face were melting. Andy felt his own face grow warm and red, but as his thoughts turned dark and violent, the teacher started to speak.

"Can I have everyone's attention?" Mr. Sanders said from the front of the class. "We have a new student."

Andy didn't catch the girl's name. She wasn't tall and had none of the acne or chubby curves that would have placed her in the seventh or eighth grade. Her hair was long and black and shot clear to her waist. Her eyes were dark and her skin the color of his mom's coffee.

Best of all, judging from her designer jeans and impractical shoes, she was not from the valley. She was new, probably from Port Cascade or even Seattle, and unlike every other student in the town of West Bend, she would know nothing about Andy or his illness.

She walked right toward Andy and the empty desk behind him. As she passed, she noticed his ruined painting and said, "Wow, cool painting. Very abstract."

Andy nodded, unsure what the new girl had meant by the comment. He was, however, certain of two things: the knot in his stomach had vanished, and his painting was done. He would not make another brush stroke.

CHAPTER THREE

Home

"What was her name?" Hector asked.

"I don't know," Andy replied. "I never did catch it. My hearing is still blinky. Did I mention she liked my painting?"

"Yeah, a dozen times. What's she look like?"

"Long black hair. I think she's Native American, or Indian, or maybe Latina. Whatever she is, she's new. She knows nothing about my illness. I'm not *cancer boy* to her."

The boys walked back through the forest, no longer encumbered with the musical instruments they had left in the school band room. The trail opened at the entrance to their neighborhood. A stone sign that once read *Pine Crest Manor*, was missing so many letters that it now read *P est Man*.

The small houses beyond were hardly manors. The lawns were neatly trimmed and flower beds budding from spring rain, but some houses needed a fresh coat of paint and others needed much more.

"You need to talk to her before someone else clues her in," Hector advised. "If you talk to her first and she sees you're just a normal kid, then it doesn't matter what anyone else says."

"Exactly. It would be nice to have a new friend."

"Hey."

"Sorry, Hector. You know what I mean."

"Yeah, I know."

Andy's house was three doors up Otter Lane. The front lawn led past his mom's rose bushes to a wide porch.

Andy stopping short, "Oh, criminy!"

"What?"

"Reggie. He called me out like you said he would. I was supposed to meet him at Founder's Park so he could kick my butt. I totally forgot."

"He's gonna be double-pissed now. You should skip school tomorrow."

"I can't just skip school. I'd miss my chance to talk to the new girl."

"You have to skip or Reggie will kill you," Hector said. "I got an idea. Tell your mom Reggie hurt you in the fight."

"I can't do that. She'd freak out."

"Exactly. She'd freak out and keep you home tomorrow."

Andy stared at the front door, dreading what lay beyond it. "She'd keep me home for a month. She barely lets me walk to school with you. She can never know about the fight."

"What if she already knows?" Hector said. "You want me to come in with you?"

"No. It'll be fine. The school nurse promised she wouldn't tell her what happened."

"Okay. See you tomorrow then. Or maybe I won't if you decide to skip."

"I won't skip."

"Then hope for a miracle."

Hector walked on up the street. Andy crossed the lawn to the front porch. He wondered if Reggie was even now waiting in Founder's Park, plotting some additional torment for having been stood up. Andy shrugged off the idea and opened the front door.

"I'm home," he said.

"Andrew McBean!" his mom shouted in reply.

She was all the way in the back kitchen, but the tone of her voice froze Andy in his tracks. His mom only called him *Andrew* when he was in trouble. He wracked his memory to identify which offense she had learned about. Was it the video game he'd borrowed from Hector's big brother? The movie he downloaded from the internet? It couldn't be the fight. She couldn't possibly know about the fight.

"Andrew Jefferson McBean!"

She knew about the fight.

She only used his middle name when it was deadly serious. The nurse! The school nurse must have told her about the fight even though she had promised not to. The front door was still open. Andy considered making a run for it. He could spend the afternoon at Hector's, but that would only delay the inevitable, so he bolted up the stairs, taking them two at a time.

Down the hall, the sign on his bedroom door read, "Stay Out: Private Property." His family hardly needed the warning, for his room disgusted his mom and mystified his dad. Opening the door revealed a chaotic mess of dirty clothes, smelly socks, and muddy boots.

Andy made his way across the floor, stepping around piles of clothes, broken toys, unfinished models, and things he had found in the garbage that might come in handy someday. Even the ceiling was crowded with Andy's collection of airplane and spaceship models, each dangling from a thin strand of clear fishing line. Over the window, a stiff gray sock hung from the curtain rod. Andy had no idea how it got there, but felt such an ambitious sock should not be disturbed.

He flopped onto his unmade bed and braced himself for the inevitable. A baseball bat hidden in the sheets jabbed him in the back. He tugged it free and tossed it aside as the door flew open. His mom stood in the doorway, her expression a mix of concern and disgust. Dara McBean was tall with auburn hair and piercing green eyes. With her hands set firmly on her hips, she presented an imposing silhouette.

"What's this about you getting into a fight?" she asked.

"The nurse promised not to tell you."

"So, it's true?"

"She promised!"

Dara made her way to his bed, stepping over and around

the more toxic items on the floor. She felt Andy's forehead and cheeks, then studied his mouth and eyes. She ran her fingers through his unruly head of hair, hoping to restore some order to the chaos. The tangled locks sprang back into disarray the moment she let go.

"You need a haircut. And you're cold and wet."

"I've been walking in the rain," Andy replied. "If you don't want me to be cold and wet, we should move someplace warm where it doesn't rain so much."

"You look flushed."

"I'm fine."

"Did this other boy hurt you?"

"Yes… No. Mrs. Russell broke it up."

"Were you hit? Did he hit you?"

"Uhhh…"

"Where did he hit you?"

Andy pointed to his chin. The red mark had faded hours ago, but his mom leaned in for a closer examination.

"You stay here. I'm calling Doctor Hilyard."

"Mom…"

"No whining. You know this is serious. And look at this room. No wonder you're not feeling well."

"I'm feeling fine!"

Dara made her way back across the room and vanished down the hall. It was no use. Her mind was made up and no amount of pleading would change it. Andy listened to the rain tapping against the window and wondered if the world could be any more dull and colorless. He studied the models hanging from the ceiling. His father had brought him the first one when he started treatment. As the weeks in the hospital turned to months, Andy finished one kit after another. When he was too weak to glue parts together, his roommate, Paul, would finish the kits for him and hang them from the ceiling of their hospital room.

Paul was a year old than Andy and an old pro at what he called the *cancer racket*. He had been treated for recurrent lymphoblastic leukemia not once, not twice, but three times. He was on a first name basis with all the doctors and nurses and, through a network of cooperative orderlies, was able to smuggle in hamburgers and milk shakes when the cafeteria food was especially disgusting.

The moment the coast was clear, Paul would hop out of his bed and wheel the I.V. stand tethered to his arm over to Andy. He taught Andy card tricks, the difference between a full house and a royal flush, and when to raise and when to fold. In return, Andy taught Paul how to make models and made up stories of crawling inside them and rocketing to a warm planet where there was no illness or pain.

Andy smiled at the memory and wished Paul were around to help pass the time. He settled at his desk for an afternoon of model-making, knowing that only his dad could free him from his bedroom prison. Hours later, as the gray skies turned black, Andy heard his dad walk up the stairs, down the hall, and knock on his door.

"Andy?"

"Come in."

The door swayed open, but Martin McBean just leaned against the frame, reluctant to set foot inside the messy room. He shared Andy's wide eyes and unruly head of brown hair. He wore gray jeans, a collared shirt, and a rugged coat. Today must have been a job-site day, when he visited the muddy locations of the buildings he helped build. On client days, he wore a tie and sport coat to met with people at his office in downtown West Bend.

"You got into a fight?" he asked.

"It was hardly a fight. Barely a scuffle. Not even a fracas. More like a skirmish."

"How did this skirmish happen?"

"Reggie Grant called me *cancer boy*. So I rammed him with my trombone."

A smirk flickered across his dad's face. It lasted only a moment, then was gone, replaced by the familiar stern look of concern. "You okay? Did you get bruised?"

"Dad…"

"This is serious. Answer me."

"Yes, but I'm better now. Though mom went off the deep end. Put me to bed and called Doctor Hilyard."

"He always said you were a fighter, but this probably isn't what he had in mind," Martin said, making his way across the room to Andy's desk. "You know your mom gets that way cause she cares about you. She's looking out for you."

"She treats me like I'm still sick, but I'm better now."

"Then prove it. Ignore people that call you names. Or go to a teacher. But don't ram people with your trombone."

Andy decided to change the subject. "I was thinking about Paul. I'd like to go see him."

"We went over there just a few weeks ago."

"I know, but I was thinking about him."

"We'll see. Now let's get washed up. Dinner's almost ready and I want to watch the news. Something happened on Mars."

Been'Tok watched the bright blue planet grow large in the view screen of the Masters' ship. A small gray planet floated nearby, but he knew that sphere was of no interest to Tarak'Nor. They hadn't abandoned the dusty red planet for a dusty gray one.

The whole spaceship was a hive of activity as Workers checked equipment and prepared for landing. The Masters' enormous faces appeared in giant holograms, barking sharp commands. The Guardians poked and prodded the Workers with muscular arms and menacing glares.

It was all Been'Tok's fault. Mounted on the small machine he had found was a diagram of the solar system with special focus on the third planet from the sun. Been'Tok had wanted to study the machine and learn more about the beings who sent it, but three Guardians arrived and took the device from him. He was a Worker, after all, and curiosity was not part of his job description. Only Masters could be curious.

Soon the orders came to dismantle the Vaporator and prepare to leave the red planet. The reason was now obvious. With his largest eye, Been'Tok could see the blue planet's atmosphere swirled with clouds, a clear indication of abundant water below. It would take months for the Vaporator to process it all, maybe years. There was enough water to fill a thousand tankers, enough for everyone on their dry home world to drink their fill.

But with so much water there must be life, and mining water from planets with advanced life was against the rules. As Been'Tok pondered this dilemma, he knew that even now the Masters were searching for the wettest place to land.

CHAPTER FOUR

Lights in the Sky

Monday's were taco night at the McBean house. It was Andy's favorite meal because the entire family made dinner together. His mom sprinkled seasoning over simmering hamburger. His dad chopped lettuce and tomatoes. Andy grilled tortillas, and even little Freddie, just five years old, grated a mound of cheese.

Andy loved tacos. Seated at the dining table, the television glowing nearby, Andy was halfway through his third one when he asked, "What's abstract?"

His father mumbled something, his mouth full, but his eyes never left the television where Anchor Dirk Rockler delivered the evening news.

"Lots of things are abstract," Dara said.

"No, I mean the word. What's it mean?"

"How was it used?" she asked.

"In art class, this girl called my painting 'abstract.'"

"A girl, huh?"

"Mom, can we stick to the subject?"

"Andy likes a girl," Freddie teased.

"Shut up, dork."

"No name calling," Dara said firmly.

"Shhh, listen," Martin said, spraying bits of taco. "They're talking about Mars."

Everyone fell quiet, as they always did when there was a story about space exploration on television. Martin was an engineer, and though his job was to make sure buildings didn't fall down, the same skills were used to launch rockets and satellites.

Dirk Rockler sat behind the Action News desk, his hair perfect and smile blinding. Rockler was always smiling. Even when the news was sad he would smile, showing off his dazzling teeth. Over his right shoulder floated a picture of Mars and the roving robot NASA had sent there.

"NASA has confirmed they are unable to contact the Mars Rover and assume it is lost," Rockler reported. "Scientists at the Jet Propulsion Lab in Pasadena speculate the probe burned up while entering the Martian atmosphere, suffered a meteor strike, or crashed on landing."

"Shoot," Martin said. "All that work and it just burns up."

He shut off the television and crunched another bite of taco. A quiet settled over the dining table, with just the clinking sound Dara made as she cut up Freddie's food.

"Don't feel bad about that Mars Rover," she said. "Science doesn't advance in a straight-line, one step after another.

There are setbacks. I'm rather proud of that little machine. Imagine making it all the way to Mars. Maybe it didn't make it to the surface, but I'm sure it taught us a lot and we'll do even better next time. Nothing worth achieving is easy."

Andy's mom was full of such handy phrases. She always said just the right thing to put everything in perspective. Andy felt the time was right. He had cleaned his plate. The television was off and no longer a distraction. Even the disappointing news about the Mars probe might encourage a positive response.

He straightened up in his chair and said, "I was thinking of trying out for soccer."

The room felt silent. Knives and forks were stilled. Freddie froze mid-chew.

"Absolutely not," Dara said.

"Mom…"

"No."

Martin cleared his throat. "Hon, maybe it's time…"

"No."

Her voice was firm. Her head tilted at the angle that told everyone further protest was futile. Andy slumped, defeated. There would be no soccer this season, maybe not even through the summer. He cleared his plate, then trudged upstairs to his room and flopped onto his bed. This time his skateboard jabbed him in the ribs. He pulled it from under a blanket and tossed it aside, wondering when he'd be allowed to ride it again.

Staring at the model spaceships swaying overhead, he imagined climbing into one, starting its engines, and rocketing through a black hole to emerge a year ago before cancer had changed his life. Closing his eyes, he could almost hear the roar of the rocket's engines and feel them rattle his bed as it soared into space.

His eyes shot open. The noise and shaking were real!

The roar outside sounded like a hundred garbage trucks rumbling down Otter Lane. Every hanging model swayed and rattled. A World War II bomber slammed into a Saturn V rocket, snapping its line and sending it crashing to the floor. Andy scrambled off his bed in time to catch another falling model, but the shaking sent more crashing, too many to save.

Strangest of all was the brilliant green glow that flickered across the window curtains. He pulled them aside. There were no garbage trucks on the street below, just Mr. Anders and his dog, Bucky. Both stood in the middle of the street, staring at the sky, bathed in the strange green light.

Their shadows danced and stretched then shrank as the lights passed overhead. Andy looked up to the dark clouds. Something flared beyond them like a car's headlights on a foggy night. A high-pitched whine filled his ears as another gleaming object passed overhead.

Someone grabbed him. Andy shouted, but couldn't hear his own scream over the deafening racket. His dad stood behind him, hands clamped to his shoulders. Andy watched his mouth move but couldn't hear what he said. Martin pulled him from the shaking room as the entire fleet of models crashed to the floor.

Down the stairs, Dara stood by the front door holding Freddie. The expression on his mom's face frightened Andy even more than the lights, the noise, and the strange sight of Mr. Anders and Bucky standing in the middle of the street. Martin threw open the front door, took Dara's hand, and led them all onto the front porch.

Mr. Anders was no longer alone in the street. A group of neighbors had joined him. There were the Penkowsky's from next door, the Garcia's from down the block, and even old Mr. Tamiya, who seldom left his house on the corner. The McBean's joined them and stared at the lights above the clouds.

"That's the third one!" Anders yelled.

"What are they?" Martin asked.

Anders shook his head. "Maybe some new plane? Something the Army is testing up at Pine Mountain?"

Andy wanted to say that the Pine Mountain Army Base didn't have an airfield, but another glowing object roared overhead, shaking the street under their feet. Every puddle rippled. The Garcia's mailbox flew open, releasing a cascade of bills and magazines. The noise and lights receded to the west, casting a green haze over the ridge of the valley, then vanished completely. All fell still and quiet save for the steady drip of rain.

They're heading west toward Port Cascade," Mrs. Penkowsky noted. "Not north to the airport."

"Too big for a plane," said Mr. Tamiya. "Just based on the height of these clouds and the size of those lights, it's bigger than any plane I know of."

More neighbors approached. The Henderson's from two doors down joined the group, as did Hector and his parents, and the Whitmore's, who seldom socialized with anyone on the street. This was the first time they had all been together since Andy's return from the hospital, when they made a banner that read *Welcome Home, Andy*, and gathered on the front lawn to cheer his arrival.

No one had taken the time to put on hats or coats, and the rain matted hair, dribbled down faces, and spotted glasses. Andy searched each face for a sign of reassurance, but found only panic and questions.

"What's going on?"

"Someone call the police!"

"I can't get any phone reception."

"Is there anything on the news?"

"My cable is out."

"What about the radio?"

Andy was eager to assess the damage to his model collection and check his supply of glue and paint to affect repairs. He started to the front porch, then noticed a streetlight flicker overhead. In one remarkable moment, every light on the block went out, plunging the world into darkness.

CHAPTER FIVE

The Meteor Lands

Everything went black. Windows that glowed warm just a moment before were now dark and vacant. The homes along Otter Lane were blank silhouettes against the gray clouds above. Even the familiar faces of Andy's neighbors were just fuzzy blobs.

Gasps of frustration hissed from the group like air from a bicycle tire. More than a few bad words were muttered, though Andy could not pinpoint the offenders. He felt his dad's hand tighten on his shoulder.

"C'mon, let's get out of the rain," Martin said.

By the time they reached the front porch, Andy's eyes had adjusted to the darkness and he saw a new light, coming from the east.

"Dad, look."

Against the high ridge of hills that led to the Olympic Mountains beyond, a light probed the jagged horizon. It bobbed there, floating like one of Andy's models, then grew brighter.

It was coming right at them.

The object descended through the clouds and green shafts of light flooded the street, blinding everyone. Mr. Carter gasped. Mrs. Penkowsky held her daughter tight. Bucky growled and barked. Everyone squinted and raised their hands to shield their eyes. Someone screamed.

Martin walked back into the street, still holding Andy's hand. Together they watched the bright object slam into the far side of the valley. A great plume of dust and dirt erupted. The glowing blob pierced through the debris and tumbled toward them. Again and again it crashed into the earth, then bounced and tumbled through the air. The meteor finally crashed into the Olsen's garage at the end of the block with a thundering boom and shock wave of dirty wind. It was big, as large as any house on Otter Lane, and skidded right up the hill, carving a deep trench in the street pavement.

Someone yelled, "Run!"

Shrieks and screams mingled with the noise of crunching wood and breaking glass as the meteor crushed cars, mailboxes, fences, and anything else in its path. Martin pulled Andy toward the house and through the front door. Dara and Freddie were already inside, running down the hall toward the kitchen. They all ran out the back door and across the yard, stopping only when they reached the garage that faced the alley.

They waited in the darkness and listened to the sound of crumpling metal and crunching stone. A green light washed over them as the meteor rose high over the peak of the house, teetered for a moment, then settled back and stopped for good.

The world fell silent. Andy focused all his concentration on the task of blinking. Once. Twice. Three times. He heard his father breathe. Freddie whimpered.

"Stay here," Martin said.

"Dad, no."

"I'm just going to take a look."

"We'll all go," Dara said.

"Okay, but stay behind me."

Martin led the way back into the kitchen and down the front hall. The entire house glowed as shafts of green light pierced each window. Martin opened the front door, revealing a wall of black stone crisscrossed with fissures of glowing crystal, like spatters of paint on a giant Easter egg. The boulder had come to rest right before the front porch. The house had not been damaged, but the same could not be said for the yard, now piled high around the smoking rock.

"Martin!" Mr. Anders called out. "You okay?"

"Yeah, we're fine."

"Can't say the same for my roses," Dara added.

The McBeans made their way off the porch and around the meteor, amazed at the smoldering rock that towered two stories high. Joining their neighbors in the street, they marveled at the trench the meteor had dug. Halfway down the block, a broken water main sprayed into the crevasse.

"That is one big asteroid," Mr. Tamiya said.

"Meteor," Andy corrected.

"Huh?"

"It's a meteor. They're asteroids out in space, but once they enter the atmosphere they're called meteors."

"Then that's one big meteor."

Martin studied his phone, his face lit by the glowing screen. "No service."

"Same here," Mr. Anders muttered, glancing to his own phone. "Maybe this thing clipped the cell towers."

"Good a guess as any."

Andy was drawn to the towering rock. White smoke drifted off the craggy surface. The roar of its landing had been replaced by the gentle crackle of cooling stone, and something more. Andy was almost certain he heard a noise from within. He scrambled up the dirt piled around it, his feet digging into the loose soil and creating little landslides with each step. Waves of heat radiated from the rock. Andy knelt at the rim of the crater and reached forward, eager to touch the craggy stone and feel its warmth.

Hands jerked him back.

"Hey!"

"Andrew Jefferson McBean, you stay away from that thing," his mom said sharply. "You don't know where it's been."

"It's been in outer space."

"You're in no condition to touch things from outer space. We should get you to bed."

"Mom."

"Don't *Mom* me!"

She dragged him off the dirt mound and past Martin and Mr. Anders. "Hon, I'm taking the boys inside. I don't think Andy is feeling well."

"You okay, son?"

"I feel fine."

Andy welcomed a new sound that distracted his parents. The siren and red flashing lights drew gasps of relief from the crowd. A few neighbors broke into applause as the fire truck appeared down the street. Unable to drive up Otter Lane, the engine went around the block and came down the hill from the opposite direction, halting just before the crater.

Andy watched Mr. Chen, who taught wood shop at Taggert Middle School and served as Chief of the West Bend Volunteer Fire Department, climb down from the truck.

"Hi'ya Martin," Mr. Chen said, fixing his helmet in place. "Looks like you caught a big one."

"A big one? There are more of these things?"

"Before the power went out we got word of boulders landing all over the county. One took out the gas station over on State Route Ten. Must be some sort of meteor shower."

Mr. Chen ordered one fireman to set up a hose and another to shut down the spraying water main. Andy watched the men go about their work, puzzled at Mr Chen's unusual choice of words.

Dara carried Freddie in one arm and pulled Andy back

Andy knelt at the peak of the crater and reached forward,
eager to touch the craggy stone and feel its warmth.

onto the porch. "Let's get you boys inside. You'll be sleeping in our room tonight."

Andy stole a last look at the giant meteor. "Funny how Mr. Chen said meteors have landed all over the county."

"What's so funny about that?"

"Meteors usually crash into the ground and break into a billion pieces," Andy replied. "They don't land."

CHAPTER SIX

The Center of Attention

Andy couldn't sleep. He lay wide awake in his parents' enormous bed, snug in his bright blue pajamas decorated with pictures of bears, moose, wolves, and other beasts of the forest. Freddie lay beside him, curled in a ball, snoring soundly. Andy couldn't imagine sleeping, not with an enormous meteor glowing on their front lawn.

Rain pelted the nearby window. He stared at the ceiling and wondered why his parents didn't have any models hanging from it. He knew that by the time he was grown and had a house of his own, he would have enough models to hang in every room.

He closed his eyes and recalled how the meteor had bounced and skipped across the valley like a flat stone across a lake. There was something strange about the landing, and he was certain it was a landing. Questions rattled his brain. What sort of rock bounces? And what were the strange noises coming from deep inside it? Would there be school tomorrow? Would Reggie still want to beat him up? Would he learn the name of the girl with the long black hair?

Maybe he had dreamed her too. Maybe the whole day had been a crazy dream and he would soon wake up and prepare to walk to school with Hector, playing Zoink while carrying his bulky trombone.

When he opened his eyes again, morning light filled the room. He rubbed his face and stretched. He could tell from the angle of sunlight through the windows that it was late. Why hadn't anyone woken him up? And where had Freddie gone?

He sat up, swung his legs from under the covers, and stepped into his slippers, each one shaped like the head of a moose, complete with furry antlers. Scampering down the stairs, he threw open the front door, eager to see the meteor in the light of day.

It stood like black wall of rock just beyond the porch. Smoke no longer rose from its many crevices, but they still glowed green. Random ticks and clicks continued to echo from the meteor, now joined by the sound of people. Lots of people. Hundreds of people. All staring at Andy.

"Look at the boy," someone yelled.

"Check out those pajamas," someone else laughed.

"Oh, he's adorable."

"Quick, take his picture."

"Hah, look at those slippers."

"Antler slippers!"

"Say cheese."

Andy rubbed his face, scratched his hair, wiped his eyes, and gaped at the scene before him. The crater had been surrounded by crime scene tape and two police officers kept the crowd back. The fire truck was right where Mr. Chen had parked it and several kids climbed upon it for a better view. The entire neighborhood surrounded the meteor, many holding phone cameras. They were taking his picture! In his pajamas and moose-head slippers! He was paralyzed with embarrassment and it only got worse.

"Nice pajamas, McBean!"

Reggie and his friends stood by the fire truck at one edge of the mob. Before Andy could reply, hands grabbed him from behind and pulled him back inside.

"Andy McBean, what are you doing?" his mom asked.

"Checking on the meteor."

"Go get dressed then have some breakfast."

"What about school?"

"The power is still out. No school today."

Andy smiled and marched up the stairs. No school. Could there possibly be two better words? No walk through the drippy forest. No struggle to stay awake in class. No having to evade Reggie and his posse. He would not be able to talk to the new girl, but no one else would either. And he could spend the entire day learning what "abstract" meant and coming up with witty remarks that would show her he was neither contagious nor radioactive. Clearly, the miracle

Hector had hoped for had come in the form of a large glowing meteor.

Filled with energy, Andy hurried to his room and selected the day's clothes from those scattered on the floor, hanging off his chair, and piled in the closet. Once dressed, he bounded downstairs to the kitchen where he made himself a bowl of cereal. The milk from the dark refrigerator was lukewarm, but still tasted sweet.

"This is the best day ever!" he shouted.

"This is not the best day ever," Dara replied. "The power is out. Everything in the freezer is thawing. Half the neighborhood is trampling what's left of our front lawn."

As Andy raised a spoonful of cereal to his mouth, a new sound caught his ears. The murmurs of the crowd outside had turned to gasps and shouts. He bolted from the table and made it out the back door before his mom could shout, "Andy McBean, you get right back here!"

Safely outside, he ran around the house and back to the front yard, the buzzing din growing louder with each step. He pushed his way through the crowd and found the source of the commotion was a news van from Channel Seven. The side door slid open, revealing Dirk Rockler, who looked even taller than he did on television. Despite the steady breeze, not a hair on Rockler's head moved. He flashed a toothy smile, eliciting a chorus of cheers and applause.

"Hello there," Rockler said to no one in particular. "Looks like we have a story here."

The crowd parted for him as he made his way to the crater. A short woman followed, struggling to carry a heavy camera and tripod. Rockler ducked under the crime scene tape without a second thought. Such barriers may discourage normal citizens, but not Dirk Rockler.

He marched up the mound of dirt and posed, hands on hips, as though he had reached the summit of Mount Everest. "How's this?" he asked the struggling camerawoman.

"That's great, Mr. Rockler," she replied.

Andy beamed. Never before had anything remotely newsworthy happened on his street. Two years ago the Penkowsky's cat, Mr. Buttons, got stuck in a storm drain, but that only rated a small mention in the West Bend Gazette. This was different. This was Dirk Rockler, anchor of the Channel Seven news in Port Cascade, standing right on what was left of Andy's front yard.

Someone grabbed Andy from behind.

"Mom!" he shouted.

"Guess again, butt brain."

Andy gulped. "Oh, hi Reggie."

Reggie shoved him against the fire truck. He was flanked by Ben, Lance, and Lori, all wearing black. "Where were you? I waited in the park and you didn't show."

"Uh... something came up," Andy stammered. "And then something came down."

"Just 'cause an asteroid lands in your yard doesn't change things. I'm still gonna kick your butt."

"Meteor."

"What?"

"It's a meteor. It's only an asteroid until it hits the earth's atmosphere. Then they're called…"

"Are you making fun of me?"

"No, I was just…"

"Andy!" a voice called.

Reggie released him, but jabbed a finger into his chest. "This isn't over, McBean."

Reggie and his crew faded into the crowd as Martin appeared around the far end of the fire truck. "There you are. How would you like to be on television?"

Martin led Andy through the crowd to the wall of the crater. Dirk Rockler, still standing high on the rim, waved for them to come forward. A police officer lifted the crime scene tape so they could duck underneath. Scrambling up the mound, Andy felt the eyes of the crowd upon him.

People had stared at him before, but never like this. In the hospital, as his hair fell out, doctors and nurses stared with fixed smiles and damp eyes. Back in West Bend, as his hair grew from stubble to rangy, teachers and students stared with relief and apprehension. Now the faces before him wore smiles and grins and raised phones to take his picture. No camera was larger than the one handled by the camerawoman, and she trained the giant lens right at him.

"Don't worry, young man," said Rockler. "That camera doesn't bite. I'll just ask you and your dad a couple questions."

The camera woman held up an open hand, then dropped fingers as she counted down, "Five, four, three…"

"This is Dirk Rockler at the scene of an amazing event," Rockler said in his booming voice, teeth sparkling in the morning light. "Last night, dozens of large meteors landed across the county, one right here in West Bend. We are joined by Martin and Andy McBean, now proud owners of a most unusual lawn ornament. Mr. McBean, tell us what happened."

Martin cleared his throat and said, "Well, last night my son, Andy, saw some strange lights in the sky and we heard this weird sound."

"What did it sound like?"

"Sort of like a machine spinning, like a car with a bad fan-belt."

"And the lights?"

"There was a bright green glow above the clouds. Never got a clean look at them until this one landed."

"And quite a landing it was," Dirk interrupted. "Let's pan over to show the folks at home the giant trench this object created as it skidded up the street."

The camerawoman panned to the deep trench. Like a crack in the earth, the pit ran all the way down the street to the splintered remains of the Olsen's garage. In the light of day, the pit appeared wider and longer than it had the night before. Great hunks of pavement were piled to either side, and one car had fallen in and now rested upside down.

"Quite a path of destruction," Dirk Rockler continued in the serious voice he used to report fires and car accidents. "You must have been horrified."

"It was pretty frightening, Dirk," Martin said. "Fortunately it only tore up the street, and the Olsen's down the block were thinking of remodeling their garage anyway."

Rockler pointing the microphone right in Andy's face. "And you, young man, what do you make of all this?"

Andy gulped, caught off guard. The camera's large eye stared right at him. He stared back, cross-eyed. The crowd leaned forward to hear what he would say, but his tongue felt swollen and his lips moved in slow-motion.

"Guh… deh…"

"What's that?" Rockler asked.

Andy scanned the crowd. One face caught his eye. He recognized the long black hair. It was the new girl from art class. She stood atop Mr. Anders' fence for a better view.

"Tuh…" Andy stammered.

"Hold that thought young man," Rockler interrupted. "Something's coming this way."

Rockler pulled the microphone away from Andy's face. The camerawoman whipped the camera around, pointing the giant lens up the street. Everyone turned to the rumbling noise coming down the hill. The mechanical sound was not unlike the whine the meteors had made, and it was coming closer.

The rough landing made Been'Tok dizzy and tired. The queasy feeling reminded him to never eat before entering a strange planet's atmosphere. But there was no time for rest or recuperation. There was work to be done. Gorn'Mek, the Guardian assigned to their crew, barked orders at Been'Tok and his fellow Workers. The Seeker must be assembled and tested before they could leave the confines of the landing shell.

The world Been'Tok saw through the shell's crystal fissures was filled with life, some of it almost certainly advanced. Birds flew in tight, acrobatic formations. Four legged animals wore bright collars with bits of jangling metal. Bipedal creatures occupied dwellings built in orderly rows.

The bipeds were not a very impressive species, each equipped with only two legs, two arms, and two small eyes. Most had just a meager clump of fur on their heads and some didn't even have that.

One biped stood out from the rest. It had bright eyes and a respectable mound of fur on its head. Most striking were its garments. They were brightly colored and adorned with drawings of wild beasts. Been'Tok knew from the many planets he had visited, that warriors often decorated their robes with the images of vanquished foes. This biped even wore the heads of horned animals upon its feet. Judging from how the other bipeds raised their voices in respect and adoration, this individual must be a great warrior among its people.

The bipeds were clearly advanced and Been'Tok dutifully reported this to Gorn'Mek, who notified the Masters. Tarak'Nor's holographic head appeared almost instantly and declared the bipeds insignificant. The Master ordered them to launch the Seeker and capture this Great Warrior as quickly as possible.

CHAPTER SEVEN

The Tripod

The ominous rumbling shook the entire neighborhood. Car alarms blared a chorus of anxiety. Up the street, a convoy of dark green trucks appeared, each carrying soldiers and equipment. The army had arrived from the Pine Mountain Base.

Dread turned to relief. The crowd shouted and clapped. Several kids broke loose of their parents' grasp to meet the troops as the convoy rolled to a halt. Dirk Rockler descended from the rim of the crater and marched toward the vehicles, the camerawoman struggling to keep up. Andy's television debut ended just as suddenly as it had began.

"What's happening?" he asked his dad.

"Looks like the cavalry has arrived," Martin replied.

They made their way off the pile of debris and watched the soldiers with shiny black rifles jump out of the trucks. A stern woman stepped out of the first vehicle. Andy knew the oak leaves pinned to the front of her gleaming helmet meant she was a major. She walked past Rockler to the crater, her right hand resting on the pistol holstered to her belt.

"Good morning folks," she said. "My name is Major Claire Astin with the National Guard. The Governor has mobilized us to set up a perimeter around each meteor and safeguard the public and that's exactly what we're going to do."

A smattering of applause drifted through the crowd as the soldiers formed a ring4 around the crater, each standing smartly with their rifles at the ready. Andy could sense that everyone felt more secure with the army here. It had been an anxious night without power or phone service, and soldiers have a way of restoring confidence and order.

Dirk Rockler stepped forward and held out his microphone. "Major, I'm Dirk Rockler, Channel Seven Action News. What are these things?"

Major Astin shrugged. "We have initial reports of twenty-eight such meteors landing across the county. They are not part of any known asteroid belt, but I can assure you that the best scientists in the world are working on it. You good people have nothing to fear. The National Guard is on the job and here to protect you."

"What about the power?" someone yelled.

"Yeah, when will the power be back on?"

"Who's gonna fill in this ditch?"

"What about the water main?"

"When will the phones be working?"

"What about the schools?"

The questions tumbled from every direction. Parents were missing work and kids were missing school. Everyone wanted to know the same thing — when would life return to normal.

Major Astin raised her hands for quiet. "Folks, the power and communications networks are out all across the state, maybe the country. The Governor has declared a state of emergency. I know this is a real inconvenience, but there's no immediate danger. I recommend you all hunker down 'cause it may take a while to sort this out."

"What could have caused this?" someone asked, sparking another flood of questions.

"Should we evacuate?"

"Are we under attack?"

Astin only shook her head. "I really don't have all the answers, but we're all in this together. It's time to cinch our belts and work as a team. One for all and all for one."

She smiled, confident her inspiring words had reassured the crowd, but no one was listening to her anymore. They were watching, mouths agape, as cracks spread across the meteor behind her. The crystal fissures and coal-black stone flaked away as a low rumble echoed from deep within. The meteor was moving.

"Dad, look," Andy said.

"I see it," Martin replied.

Major Astin stared at the meteor, "Everyone get back!"

The crowd needed no encouragement. Some people ran.

Others screamed. Even the soldiers backed up a few paces. The rumbling groan from the meteor was joined by a grating sound that reminded Andy of fingernails across a chalkboard. He clamped his hands over his ears, but there was no muting the agonizing noise.

It came from the highest tip of the meteor where the jagged stone began to move counter-clockwise, revealing a seam of shiny metal that widened with each rotation. The loose cap slid free and fell into the crater with a resounding thud.

"Soldiers, maintain formation," Major Astin shouted, though her voice was drained of all confidence. "Hold the line!"

Andy leaned back against his father, reassured at his presence. It was clear the meteor resting in their front yard was no meteor at all. It was hollow. It was a machine.

Those who hadn't fled, torn between curiosity and self-preservation, gasped at the sight of something moving along the flat rim of the opening. A clump of fur, not unlike the paw of a bear, gripped the rim. Behind it rose another furry blob, this one distinguished by a large darting eye, and beneath it, a mouth in the shape of an upturned-V, saliva dripping at each corner.

Dirk Rockler stepped to the base of the crater, waving his reluctant camerawoman to follow. "This is Dirk Rockler, Channel Seven News. I am standing before a meteor that landed just outside West Bend. But this is no meteor, ladies and gentlemen. One end has opened and some form of life appears to be climbing out. I will attempt to communicate with it and in doing so become the first human in history to speak with an alien life form."

Martin pulled Andy away. "Let's go."

"But Dad…"

"No buts."

Dirk Rockler climbed up the rim of the crater. "Who are you?" He shouted to the creature. "Where do you come from? My name is Dirk Rockler."

The camerawoman trained her camera lens on the creature that stared down at Rockler, its big eye darting nervously.

Don't do that, Andy thought.

He had been on the other side of the lens just moments ago and knew how intimidating it was. Sure enough, the creature ducked below the rim of the opening.

"C'mon," Martin said.

He led the way down the side yard. Andy lost sight of Dirk Rockler and Major Astin, but caught a glimpse of a machine rising out of the hollow meteor. A silver appendage swayed over the crowd, its almond-shaped tip glowing bright green. Martin pulled Andy across the backyard as Dara ran out the back door carrying Freddie.

"What's happening?" she yelled.

"We're leaving!" Martin replied. "Get in the truck!"

They ran to the pickup parked behind the garage, and could only hear the action on the other side of the house.

A gunshot ripped the air. Someone screamed. A chorus of weapons crackled. Bullets clinked against metal. A bright light flashed, accompanied by an other-worldly scream.

Martin lifted Andy into the truck bed, then climbed behind the wheel. Dara and Freddie crammed into the small passenger seat. The pickup roared to life and lurched back into the alley. Andy rolled across the bed and when the truck surged forward, he toppled back in the opposite direction.

Flat on his back, he watched something rise above his house. It was the alien weapon, bright and shiny. Bolts of light shrieked from it, spraying the crowd below and mixing with their chorus of screams. The weapon rested on a larger body that rose on three armored legs. One leg bent at its knee and crashed through the second floor of Andy's house. The debris scattered across the backyard, joined a moment later by the crunching thud of the machine's metal foot.

It's walking, Andy thought. *The machine can walk.*

CHAPTER EIGHT

The Chase

The McBean pickup sped down the alley, away from the alien machine standing in their backyard. Andy allowed himself to breathe again, but his relief was short-lived. The tripod's silver body turned, its glowing porthole staring right at him. He pressed his back against the front of the truck bed to put as much distance between himself and the machine as possible.

The tripod stepped over what was left of the McBean house and followed the truck down the alley, each thundering step bringing the terrible weapon closer. The pickup lurched to the left at the end of the block, turning onto the main street that led out of Pine Crest Manor.

"Go, go, GO!" Andy yelled.

The truck skidded to a halt.

Andy pressed his face against the cabin window. "Dad, don't stop!"

Through the windshield he saw a tangle of cars jammed

at the neighborhood entrance. Red taillights glowed. A chorus of horns honked. No one was moving except for the alien tripod that turned out of the alley and marched right at them.

The truck lurched into reverse. Andy held on as they backed up toward the towering machine. The pickup swerved between the tripod's legs then spun around, wheels squealing, and surged up the hill. Andy rolled across the bed and slammed into the back tailgate. He watched the machine pause over the mess of jammed cars.

"Don't follow us," Andy mumbled to himself. "Just stay right there."

The glowing porthole studied the cars below, then turned toward the pickup as though trying to decide which way to go. Andy knew it was wrong, but hoped the aliens would stay amidst his neighbors' cars and leave their truck alone. As they roared up the hill, however, the machine made up its mind and marched after them.

The truck turned onto the Old Mill Road that ran along the Otter River and into the foothills beyond. The giant machine gained on them, its monstrous feet digging pits into the concrete. The weapon extending over its body glowed bright green.

"Dad, turn the truck!" Andy yelled. "Turn now!"

Martin jerked the truck off the road as the tripod shot green bolts into the pavement behind them, melting the surface into glowing ripples of asphalt. The pickup bounded onto the flat strawberry fields of the Hoffman Berry Farm. Andy bounced up and down as the truck leaped over rows of bushes, zigzagging toward the farm house and barn.

The alien machine gained on them, its plodding walk hastening to an ungainly trot. More bolts exploded from its weapon and tore into the Hoffman barn, blasting it apart. Andy ducked as chunks of burning wood and debris landed around him.

The pickup bounced across another field, the tripod now right behind it. Dangling from the machine's body was a bubble-like turret surrounded by a cluster of metal tentacles. Their tapered ends descended toward Andy and swept over his head as the truck swerved back and forth.

Then the tripod did something remarkable.

It crouched low on its three legs and jumped into the air, soaring right over the truck. Andy watched in disbelief as the towering machine flew right over him. It landed directly in front of the truck with an earth-crunching thud. The shock-wave sent a cloud of dirt and plants into the air. Andy coughed and gagged, but held tight, desperate not to be thrown out. He could no longer see the tripod but knew it was waiting straight ahead.

The truck swerved to the right.

The machine remained on the field, no doubt expecting the vehicle to emerge from the cloud at its feet. But as the dust settled, no truck appeared. The pickup had already sped back onto the Old Mill Road.

Now Andy understood why his dad had driven up the hill. The Mill Road Tunnel, cut into a massive hillside of stone, lay straight ahead. It may be the safest place in the valley. There was no way the alien tripod could fit inside, and not even its death-ray could cut through the granite cliff. Andy yearned for the tunnel's damp safety. Never before had a dark hole been so appealing. They were almost inside. Just a few more...

A burst of green energy exploded beside the truck.

The pickup bounced in a cloud of smoke and flame. Andy felt weightless and disoriented, the world spinning around him. He landed with a sudden thud in the thicket of bushes at the side of the road. Groggy and dazed, he watched the pickup disappear into the tunnel, trailing a wake of sparks into the darkness.

The tripod stopped before the tunnel opening. Its silver tentacles reached inside, but came back empty. In a fit of frustration, the machine rammed its armored body into the cliff, sending down an avalanche of boulders.

Andy watched it all from the side of the road until the woozy, dizzy feeling returned and sleep claimed him.

Been'Tok watched the Great Warrior's chariot vanish into the underground lair in a cloud of smoke and sparks. Losing the Warrior was a disappointing start to their patrol. The Masters blamed the Workers. Gorn'Mek was furious and rammed the Seeker's hull into the mountainside, burying the opening with boulders.

Been'Tok, however, marveled at the Warrior. For an insignificant life form there was something undeniably special about the creature. The Warrior was no taller than the average Worker and yet had clearly attained a position of authority in its tribe. Been'Tok wondered how a creature no bigger than himself could be a leader on this wet planet.

Perhaps the Masters were wrong about the bipeds. Maybe they were significant after all.

CHAPTER NINE

Alone

"Andy, wake up," Paul said.

"Huh? What?"

"Wake up, doofus!"

Andy squinted at the sunlight streaming through the hospital window. He'd had the strangest dream about a giant meteor skidding to a stop in his front yard and a giant alien machine climbing out. He stretched and looked around the sterile room. Paul stood at the side of his bed, leaning on his ever-present I.V. stand.

"Dude, you were having a crazy dream."

"Tell me about it," Andy replied.

He rubbed his scalp and his hand returned, covered with hair. "My hair!"

"Hey, calm down," Paul said. "It's the chemo. It happens. Didn't they tell you?"

Andy's eyes welled. "Yeah, but… my hair!"

Paul chuckled and pulled off his baseball cap, revealing

his own fuzz-covered scalp. "You thought it wouldn't happen to you, huh? Thought you were special? Yeah, I hear that. But don't worry, you can do this."

"I can't."

"Sure you can. This is nothing. Piece of cake. Walk in the park. Day at the beach."

"No!" Andy shouted, arms outstretched.

*

Andy bolted upright in a tangle of bushes. His eyes were open but he couldn't see. Rain spattered his face. His mouth was dry and he opened it to catch some drops. He wasn't in the old hospital room with Paul. He scratched his head and was relieved to feel his hair littered with leaves and mud.

He was lying in a thicket of bushes.

Then he remembered the lumbering tripod and the frantic chase across the Hoffman farm. The tunnel was just ahead of them, safe and dark, and then a blinding flash of light.

"Dad!" Andy shouted.

He was soaked and wished he'd grabbed his jacket before the alien machine attacked. He rolled onto his hands and knees, clenching the dirt to steady himself, then crawled out of the bushes and onto the road. His legs wobbled beneath him.

His vision adjusted to the darkness and, instead of black, he now saw shades of gray. The cloudy sky was the lightest gray and the cliff ahead somewhat darker. He walked toward it, but tripped over something and landed on one knee with a jolt of pain. He rose again, rubbed the scrape, and proceeded more carefully, recalling how the tripod had rammed the cliff over and over again.

All around him were rocks and boulders. What bits of pavement he could make out had been cracked and pitted by the tripod's heavy feet. Off to one side he recognized a twisted hunk of metal as the tailgate of his father's pickup. But where was the rest of it?

The tunnel.

The truck had made it into the tunnel, trailing a shower of sparks from the metal axle grinding against the road. Andy stared at the mound of boulders. He grabbed a smaller one and tugged with all his might. The stone wouldn't budge. He didn't expect it to, but felt he had to try.

His stomach churned and growled. The ache dropped him to his knees. He hadn't eaten since when? That morning? No, he'd barely started his bowl of cereal before racing from the breakfast table to watch Dirk Rockler arrive. No wonder he was hungry. He hadn't eaten since last night's tacos.

Andy stepped back from the boulders, careful not to fall into a tripod footprint, now filling with water. How long had he been unconscious? Hours?

"Dad!"

He knew yelling was useless — there was no way anyone on the other side of the rocks could hear him — but what else could he do? What could he say or do to get beyond the boulders and into the tunnel where his parents would be looking for him.

He shuddered, wet and cold, trying to devise an answer, but soon realized there was none. It was a problem without a solution. He glanced up the face of the cliff, then to the forest that stretched along its base. He knew there was a trail along the Otter River that led to the other side of the mountain, but he was in no condition for a hike. He wasn't properly dressed and had no flash light.

And he was hungry.

He gripped his rumbling belly and thought of the Hoffman farm. It was not far away and Mr. Hoffman might know what to do. Maybe he could give Andy something to eat. His stomach grumbled at the thought of food and he turned down the road, hunched against the rain.

He thought about cutting across the berry fields, but knew they would be muddy, so he stuck to the road until reaching the Hoffman mailbox. Walking up the gravel drive, he passed the remains of the destroyed barn. Blackened timbers hissed in the rain, releasing tendrils of white smoke.

The Hoffman farmhouse was completely dark, its windows like blank eyes. One winked at him as the evening breeze tugged the curtain inside. Andy stepped onto the front porch, thankful for the shelter. Wind chimes plunked a random melody. He rang the doorbell. There was no response, just the wind chimes and the sound of rain on the porch roof.

Andy remembered the power was out. That would mean the doorbell wouldn't work, so he knocked, but there was still no answer. He knocked again.

"Mr. Hoffman," he called. "Mr. Hoffman!"

Nothing. Mr. Hoffman was old and didn't walk very fast, but would have made some noise by now. Andy shivered and turned toward the porch steps. A gust of wind drove him back under cover.

It would be a long walk back home and he longed for his red jacket hanging in the front closet, and the kitchen with milk and cereal and bread and jam. That is, if the house was still there. The alien machine had crushed much of the second floor and might have destroyed the rest. What if the machine was still there, standing back in the crater that used to be his front yard?

Andy knocked again, more determined than ever to get inside. He turned the knob. Locked. He shook and jiggled it. The door didn't budge, but a line had been crossed. Andy was set on getting inside Mr. Hoffman's house. This was an emergency. If an alien invasion didn't qualify as an emergency, then what did?

The porch windows were painted shut, but he remembered the open window on the side of the house. He stepped off the porch, gusts of rain challenging every step, and found the waving curtain. The window that had been shattered by a flying piece of the wrecked barn. Andy spied a wood pallet leaning against the house and dragged it under the window.

He stepped upon it to reach inside. Careful to avoid the shards of glass still in the frame, he twisted the latch, lifted the window, and crawled inside.

Inside, he thought. *So much better than outside.*

The house was cold, but dry. Andy stood in a small room that had once been a child's bedroom, but was now used as an office. The walls were covered in flowery wallpaper. There was a desk, chairs, and a file cabinet. Papers had blown all over the floor.

The mess reminded Andy of his own bedroom, and the thought embarrassed him. He crossed to the open door, avoiding the glass scattered across the rug like bits of ice. The back hallway was even darker than the office.

"Hello," he said loudly. "Mr. Hoffman? Is anyone home? It's Andy McBean."

There was no answer. Andy headed toward the kitchen where dim light from the windows glimmered off the linoleum floor. He tried the light switch though he knew the effort would be fruitless. A clock on the wall had stopped at 8:37, the moment the power went out in the valley. The moment everything had changed.

Andy grabbed a hand towel from a hook and dried his sopping hair. A yellow phone hung on the wall by the back door. He picked up the receiver, but the line was dead. The sight of the refrigerator made his mouth water. When he opened the door, the light didn't come on, but a carton of milk was still cool to the touch. He sniffed it to be safe. It smelled like milk, but not too much like milk, so he drank right from the carton. He couldn't pour the milk down his throat fast enough and it ran over his cheeks and across his wet shirt.

He set it on the counter, saw the bread box, and smiled.

After three slices of bread and strawberry jam, and two more glasses of milk, Andy's stomach quieted, but he was still cold and wet. If there were power, he would put his clothes in a dryer until they were warm and fluffy. He wondered how people made their clothes warm and fluffy before there was electricity.

He stepped out of the kitchen, chewing a fourth slice of bread. It felt strange to walk around another person's house and look at the family photos hanging on the walls. One picture showed Mr. Hoffman as a young man, his arm around a pretty woman. Andy assumed she was Mrs. Hoffman, who had died long before Andy was born.

The picture made him think of his parents and brother. Were they buried in the tunnel? Tunnels have two entrances and it's possible they made it out the other side.

In the closet by the front door he found jackets and coats. He tugged a blue slicker off one hook. A flannel shirt hung nearby and he grabbed that as well. Pulling off his wet shirt, he let it fall to the floor with a soggy plop and pulled on the flannel shirt. It scratched his skin, but was dry and that was the important thing. The slicker was too big even with the sleeves rolled up to his wrists but would have to do.

He took a deep breath and opened the front door. The rain was steady and the sky even darker, but he knew he had to leave. Something told him he couldn't spend the night here and must make his way back home. There he would find a grown-up who would certainly know what to do.

But he closed the door.

It wasn't the rain that drove him back to the kitchen, but a sense of unfinished business. He set the dirty plate he had used in the sink and rinsed out the glass. Near the phone, he found a note pad and pencil. In the best penmanship he could muster, he wrote a note and left it under the empty milk bottle on the kitchen counter.

Satisfied, he left the kitchen, zipped up the big coat and fastened its hood snug around his head, then opened the front door and started the journey home.

CHAPTER TEN

The Survivor

It was dark by the time Andy reached his neighborhood. Not the average darkness that marked the end of each overcast day, or the dimming twilight that drained all color from the world, but the true black of a moonless sky blanketed in clouds heavy with rain.

Andy wished he had looked for a flashlight in Mr. Hoffman's kitchen. He should have known that he would need one. It was a stupid mistake and this was no time for stupid mistakes. He also wished he had pocketed the rest of the loaf of bread — his stomach was grumbling again as he walked down the main road by the *P est Man* sign.

Fires glowed here and there across the neighborhood. There was a hole in the roof of the Carter's house. Plumes of smoke billowed from the Olsen's shattered garage. A macabre tangle of cars clogged the main road. Cars, trucks, and SUVs were quiet and empty, their doors flung open. Flashing turn signals and taillights cast an ominous red glow over the scene. Andy recognized Mr. Anders sports car, the Penkowsky's station wagon, and the Moreno's minivan, which rested on its nose like a toy discarded by a giant child.

There was no sign of the alien machine that had caused the damage, though tripod footprints were all around, cracked into the pavement and dug deep into the muddy shoulder of the road. Andy turned away from the too-quiet street and hurried up the alley toward his house. The idea of home beckoned him as much as the promise of shelter.

The garage remained as they had left it that morning, but the same could not be said for the house. Half the second floor had been swiped away and the backyard was littered with wood beams and chunks of wall and roof. Andy was tempted to run to the back door, but the last thing he wanted was a rusty nail stabbing him through his tennis shoes.

He headed around the debris and down the side of the house. It was slow going and he paused once to marvel at how one corner of his home had been sheered from the rest. He had never imagined that a house could be sliced like a cube of butter.

In the front yard, the broken shell of the alien meteor rested black and quiet in the crater. The seams of crystal that once glowed bright green were now dull and dead. All around the pit, the signs of battle could be seen. Crushed cars and trucks were mingled with blobs of melted metal that had once been artillery.

Andy stopped before the front porch. A dead alien lay sprawled across the steps. It faced away from him, presenting just a large mass of brown fur encircled by a metallic device that resembled a shawl or collar. He dreaded to touch the creature's flesh, but it blocked his path to the front door, so he took hold of the metal device and tugged.

The beast tumbled off the steps. Andy leaped back as the dead thing landed at his feet, staring up at him with three dull eyes. The one in the middle was the largest, as big as a soccer ball, with baseball-sized eyes to either side. The alien carried a metal device in one hand and, in the other, a long weapon that resembled the tripod's ray-gun.

Andy stepped around the creature to the front door and darted inside. There was none of the warmth he had hoped for. Whatever heat the house once held had been sucked out the open roof. Even now rain fell upon the stairs leading to the second floor.

Andy walked back to the kitchen. The phone on the wall was dead, but his mother's phone was still plugged into the charger on the counter. Its screen glowed bright under his face, but flashed the words, "No Reception." He shoved it into the pocket of his oversized coat.

Down the front hall, the living room was undamaged and just the sight of the fireplace warmed him with the vision of the fire he would build there. He wandered upstairs, his feet squishing on the rain-soaked carpet. It was strange to look up and feel rain on his face. His hopes rose at the sight of his bedroom door, but pushing it open revealed nothing but devastation.

His room was gone.

The walls and ceiling were wiped away and he could see right across the side yard to the Penkowsky house. He used the bright screen of his mother's phone to shine a cone of light across the floor. There was nothing left, just bits and pieces, nothing that could be identified as a chair or a bed or a toy. When things are broken this badly they no longer have names. Andy tried to calculate the labor required to restore his room to the way it had been when something caught his eye beyond one missing wall.

A small blue light danced in the darkness. At first Andy thought it was a firefly and stepped across room for a closer look. The light moved back and forth in a window on the second floor of a house across the street. Andy waved his mom's phone then lowered it and waited. A moment later, the distant light waived back. Andy swung his phone up and down. The light did the same. Then he waved his phone in a circle and again the light made the exact same pattern.

Someone was in that house. Someone alive.

Andy noted the location of the house and the window, then bounded out of the room and down the stairs, nearly slipping and falling on the wet steps. He threw open the front the door and leaped off the porch, around the dead alien, and across the battlefield that had been Otter Lane. He saw the light in a window behind the Anders' home.

He cut through the Anders' back yard. The idea of trespassing would have been unthinkable just hours ago, but things had changed. His respect for property lines had vanished just like all of his neighbors.

All save one.

The Anders house appeared to have suffered no damage in the alien attack. The backyard patio with its covered trellis and mammoth barbecue was just as Andy remembered it from last summer's block party. The house behind it, however, had not fared so well.

Much like Andy's own home, part of the second floor had been destroyed, perhaps by the alien machine, or an errant shot from an army canon. Andy climbed over the Anders' fence into the back yard of the damaged home. He looked up to the window where the light had appeared.

"Hey," he yelled. "Is anyone up there?"

There was a muffled response and he could see a blue glow in the window.

"I'll be right up," he yelled.

He ran across the back yard and pulled open the screen door, which promptly fell out of its frame. Pushing it aside, he tried the back door, but it was stuck. He shoved his shoulder against it. Once. Twice. The third shove loosened the door and the fourth sent it flying open and Andy sprawling upon the kitchen floor.

He knew it was the kitchen, because the room was filled with moving boxes, each labeled "KITCHEN." He stood and walked into the dining room, stacked high with boxes marked "DINING ROOM." Whoever lived here had just moved in.

Andy used the phone to light his path to the front stairs. "Hello?" he called out.

The muffled reply drew him to the second floor. He saw a flashing light under the door at the end of the hall and rushed toward it. Pushing the door open, his first step into the dark room landed on thin air. Only by clutching the doorknob did keep from falling. He teetered over a pit of broken beams and jagged timbers before falling back into the hallway.

The floor of the room was gone. So was the ceiling and two of the four walls. The alien machine had stomped right through the roof, smashing everything into the basement two stories down. Across the abyss, a small island of floor remained beneath one window. A section of shingled roof had fallen across the perch, but a slender arm reached from behind it and waved a glowing phone back and forth.

"Careful," said the voice across the chasm.

CHAPTER ELEVEN

A Dangerous Rescue

A ndy kneeled in the door frame and stared at the waving arm on the far side of the pit. There was no way down from the high perch. The chasm was littered with jagged beams, broken furniture, and crushed moving boxes labeled, "BASEMENT," "LIVING ROOM." and "CHARLIE."

"Over here," called the voice.

"I see you," Andy replied. "Don't move. Stay right there."

"Duh. If I could go somewhere, I wouldn't be here."

"My name's Andy. Are you Charlie?"

"Yeah, how'd you know?"

"The moving boxes. Your name's on them."

"Oh, right. Can you get help?"

"No, I can't. Everyone's gone."

"Everyone?"

"Everyone."

The realization struck Andy like a cold breeze. On the walk home he assumed he would find at least one grown-up in his neighborhood, someone to provide answers and provide guidance. The world was broken and putting things back together was what grown-ups are best at. Almost any adult would do, but the simple fact that a kid named Charlie had spent the whole day trapped above a pit told Andy no help was coming any time soon.

"Then you'll have to do it," Charlie said.

"Do what?"

"Help me. Can you get a ladder from the garage?"

Andy shined his phone out the shattered side of the house toward the crushed remains of the garage. "I think it's broken."

"The ladder?"

"No, the garage."

Andy watched Charlie's arm extend from behind the fallen chunk of roof. She waved her phone across the pit below. "What about those beams?"

"What about them?"

"Duh. Find one long enough to reach across the pit. Do I have to draw you a picture?"

"Oh, right. I get it. I'll be right back. Wait here."

"Again... not going anywhere."

Andy ignored the snarky reply and ran back down the hall and down the stairs. Off the front hallway, he stopped before what was left of the living room. It was directly beneath

Charlie's room and everything in it had been smashed through the floor and into the basement.

Andy saw a wooden beam about ten feet long and eight inches wide. He grabbed one end and pulled it from the wreckage. It was heavy, and one side was barbed with twisted nails, but the other side was smooth and just might work. He dragged the beam up the stairs, the trailing end clumping over each step, and pulled it down the hall to the open bedroom door.

"I'm back," Andy said.

"And I'm still here," Charlie replied.

"I found a piece of wood you can crawl across."

"That won't work."

Andy pushed the beam out through the door. "Sure it will. You just crawl along this beam to the door."

"That's not the problem. The problem is I'm stuck. You have to come over here."

"What?"

One arm grabbed the fallen section of roof and pushed. The shingles rattled, but didn't budge. "See?" Charlie said. "I can't push this junk out of the way. You have to come over here and help me."

Andy stopped pushing the beam. It was one thing to help Charlie to crawl to safety, but quite another to risk his own life and join her on a precarious perch. He considered going to look for help. There must be someone hiding in a basement or garage or... somewhere.

He pushed the beam farther out over the pit and was soon putting

all his weight on the near end to keep it from falling.

No, he decided. *I am the help.*

"Okay, I'm coming over," Andy said.

"Any time this week."

He pushed the beam farther across the pit and soon leaned all his weight on the near end to keep it from falling. When the far end reached the small island of floor, and both ends rested firm, he took a deep breath and crawled onto the beam.

It held his weight.

Encouraged, he put his left hand ahead of his right. The beam creaked, and he waited for it to settle. The next step placed all his weight on the beam. He wondered if this was really such a good idea, but took a breath and crawled forward.

The beam swayed, but held.

Andy wondered how many steps lay ahead of him. Should he try to hurry across the beam, or go slowly? The creaking answered the question for him. Looking back, he saw that end slip an inch toward the abyss. The beam was sagging under his weight, pulling both ends down. He thought about going back, but it was just as far as to go forward.

Andy crawled another step and then another. The beam groaned as though in pain. He felt it slide again and knew it wouldn't hold much longer. In a quick series of steps, he crawled the final distance across the pit and onto the small section of floor. There was barely enough room for him to stand, but he welcomed every square inch.

His nerves were as wobbly as the beam that still shuddered over the pit. Charlie's hand reached out from behind the fallen slab of roof and tugged at his pant leg.

"Okay, let's do this," she said. "Push on three."

Andy took hold of the roof and braced his back against the wall. "One, two, three, PUSH!"

They both pushed with all their might, but the chunk of plywood and shingles only budged an inch. Andy paused and shook the soreness from his hands.

"One more time," he said. "PUSH!"

They gripped the wood and pushed. Rafters creaked and groaned. Nails squealed as they were pulled from beams. Suddenly, the chunk broke free and tipped into the pit. Andy watched helplessly as it fell right onto the narrow beam he had just crawled across, snapping it like a twig.

Everything fell into the pit with a thundering crash. Andy toppled forward, carried by his own momentum. He teetered on the balls of his feet, when someone grabbed him from behind and pulled him back to safety. He leaned against the wall, catching his breath. When he opened his eyes, he thought he might be dreaming. Standing beside him was the girl from his art class.

"Hey, you're the kid with the asteroid," she said.

"You're in my art class. You're Charlie?"

"Yeah. Short for Charlene, but if you ever call me that, I will break you."

Given the way she glared at him, Andy didn't doubt her

for a minute. Her dark eyes made him uncomfortable, but he couldn't stop looking at them. She was a mess, her face smudged and dirty, and her long hair littered with bits of debris. The chunk of roof had kept her dry, but her clothes were covered in dust. He wondered if he looked as messy and ran his hands through his hair, wishing he had a mirror.

Charlie stared into the pit. "Shoot, we lost the beam."

"Now what?"

Charlie tilted her head back. Andy studied her neck, then followed her gaze to the top of the wall behind them and the flaps of asphalt shingles draped over the edge. Rain dripped steadily, not enough to soak them, but more than enough to be annoying.

"If we can't climb down maybe we can go up on the roof," Charlie said.

"Yes, good idea. Give me a boost."

"Why should I give you a boost? It was my idea. You give me a boost."

"'Cause I can pull you up after I get up there. Can you pull me up?"

She stared at him, perhaps trying to decide if she could pull him up, when the floor shuddered. The whole house swayed, the walls rocking. Andy and Charlie braced themselves as a distant sound grew louder, bringing with it the trauma and dread of the day. Several blocks away, the alien tripod marched toward them, its searchlights cutting beams through the rainy mist.

CHAPTER TWELVE

Escape in the Night

The crunching footfalls of the alien tripod spread tremors across the neighborhood, up the walls of Charlie's shattered house, and right through Andy's body. Cracks rippled across the wall behind him.

"We have to get out of here," he said.

"Really? You think?" Charlie replied. "Cause I was just getting settled in."

"Make a step."

"Huh?"

Andy demonstrated how to make a step. Charlie nodded and laced her fingers together. Andy set one muddy shoe into them and reached up the wall. The house shuddered again. Walls cracked and wallpaper ripping in jagged tears. The tripod's searchlights swept the neighborhood, flashing through the broken window.

"Hurry," Charlie shouted.

"Almost there. Higher."

Charlie groaned and lifted. The house rattled again, the plaster cracks splitting wider. Andy could feel the rough shingles of the roof. He reached over the edge and pulled himself up as Charlie pushed from below. With one elbow hooked onto the roof, he could see the tripod just blocks away, its armored body glistening wet and floodlights searching back and forth.

Andy had no intention to be found. He wriggled his body upon the roof and swung his legs up over the edge so that he lay flat on the damp shingles. The house rattled again and he felt the structure buckle beneath him. The whole place was falling apart. Twisting himself around, he reached back over the edge. Charlie stretched up to him, her eyes filled with fear. Their fingers curled about one another until their hands locked together.

The house trembled.

The small island of floor beneath Charlie's feet buckled and collapsed.

"No!" she shouted, dangling over the pit, nothing but Andy's hand to hold her.

The tremors stopped, but only because the alien machine had turned toward the sound of her scream. Searchlights cut through the rain and blinded Andy. He pulled with all his might, lifting Charlie up the wall. She gripped the edge of the roof. Andy let go of her hands and took hold of her belt. He pulled until she flopped onto the shingles beside him, gasping for breath.

"Let's go," she said.

She scrambled to the chimney as the machine marched toward them. Andy followed right behind. Charlie pulled him behind the brick tower as the tripod's searchlights swept over the house. She tugged his sleeve and led the way over the peak of the roof and down the other side, to an open gabled window.

It was the second window Andy had climbed through that day, and this time he tumbled across a night stand, crashing a lamp to the floor. The room was dark, but he heard Charlie's voice.

"This way," she called, already out the door.

He staggered after her, the tripod's footfalls shaking the floor and filling his ears. He hurried down the same stairs he had ran up just minutes ago and followed Charlie out the front door. She led him to the bushes at the corner of the house, beneath a large tree.

They pressed themselves low and flat against the house as the alien spotlight washed over the front yard. Through the branches of the tree they watched the giant body of the machine step over the roof. One metal foot smashed through the chimney and landed on the street before them.

Don't move, Andy thought. *Don't even breathe.*

The machine's body swayed overhead on its slender legs. Andy heard a chorus of voices drift down to him. He thought it was just his blinky hearing at first, but searching through the tree branches, he saw the faces of people. They were trapped in a cage hanging from the belly of the machine. Bars of light rotated around them.

A man spied them through the tree branches and yelled, "Run! Get out of here before they grab you!"

Andy cocked his head, puzzled at the idea of being *grabbed* by the machine. He had seen the tripod crawl out of its shell, blast the army with its ray gun, stomp across the neighborhood, and even leap over the family pickup, but he had never seen it grab anything.

"The tentacles," Andy whispered, recalling the metal appendages that tried to pluck him out of the truck.

"What tentacles?" Charlie asked.

As if to answer her question, the machine's dangling appendages reached toward them. Their tapered ends wandered across the yard. One wrapped itself around the mailbox, yanking the wooden post right out of the ground. Another slithered over the top of a parked car and smashed the windshield to probe inside.

Charlie tugged Andy's coat sleeve. She pulled him to the right, but one tentacle felt its way into their path. They retreated to the left, but another pawed at the tree before them. It coiled itself around the trunk and pulled. Branches swayed and roots burst forth from the soil and ripped across the surrounding lawn. Andy knew if the machine toppled the tree, they would be exposed to the beings inside. Charlie gasped and he took hold of her arm and held tight.

A frightened shriek drew everyone's attention.

Down the street, a man ran out of a house and across the yard. The tentacles instantly let go of the tree, the mailbox, and the car. The tripod rose to its full height and plodded down the road, catching up to the poor man in four thundering strides.

A tentacle whipped out with remarkable speed and coiled itself around the man's legs, sweeping him aloft. It held the screaming man upside down before its glowing portholes, then deposited him into the cage with the other captives.

Andy had seen enough and pulled Charlie along the wall of the house away from the machine and its latest victim. They ran from shadow to shadow, through the darkness and rain, toward home.

It was the Great Warrior. Been'Tok was certain of it. From his perch in the Grabber turret he had a clear view of the two bipeds hiding beneath the large plant and he recognized the Warrior's face and wild fur.

But how could this be? How could the Warrior be standing against the dwelling next to another biped with long black fur? The entrance to its underground lair had been sealed by an avalanche of boulders. Was there more than one Warrior? Did he have some special powers of teleportation? Did the lair have another exit?

Yes, that must be it. The lair must have another exit. The bipeds were clever, which meant they were intelligent, which meant they were significant. Been'Tok should report this to Gorn'Mek, but something told him the Masters would not agree. In all the worlds they had visited, the Masters had never deemed any of the life forms they found significant enough to stop processing.

Been'Tok made a decision. He would not report the Great Warrior. He would not follow the rules this time. It was a small act of rebellion and filled him with a feeling that was both pleasant and unfamiliar. There was no word for the feeling and he made a note to invent one.

Thankfully, another biped appeared some distance away, drawing everyone's attention. This creature was neither a fighter nor a skilled runner, and Been'Tok easily plucked him from the street with one deft swipe of a Grabber.

Gorn'Mek was satisfied with the capture and directed Been'Tok to place the biped in the holding pen with their other captives. The Seeker marched through the darkness back to the cluster of structures at the mouth of the valley. Been'Tok grinned the whole way, satisfied at his decision to let the Warrior go.

CHAPTER THIRTEEN

Fire and Food

A ndy and Charlie took the long way back to his house. They crept slowly, peering around corners and staying close to cover, just in case the tripod returned. Along the way, Andy learned three things. First, that Charlie's phone didn't have any reception either. Second, the power was out across the entire neighborhood — every street was dark and silent. And third, Charlie liked to talk.

"We need food," she said, crouching behind a parked car. "I'm starving. I haven't had anything to eat since that thing stepped on my house. We need food and shelter. Not necessarily in that order. Is your house okay? Doesn't really matter. We can take our pick of houses. Stuff to eat in all of them, I'm sure."

"Mine is…"

"And a fire. We need a fire. I'm freezing. Trapped like that all day. At least I had some cover, or I'd be freezing *and* wet. On the other hand, if that piece of roof hadn't trapped me,

94

I'd have found a way to climb down. I'm a good climber. What happened to you? I ran as soon as that thing came out of that asteroid."

"It's not a…"

"Did you run? Everybody ran. Screaming and shouting. Speeding off in their cars. I could have been run over. The soldiers didn't run. I heard their guns firing. Did you hear them? Then that ray gun and more screams. I kept running. Tried to call my mom, but my phone was dead. She works at Pine Mountain? Do you know where the Pine Mountain Army Base is?"

"Sure, it's…"

"She had to work. She does computer stuff for the army. Everyone was called in. Something about Mars. That's all she told me. Top secret and all. She told me to hang out at the house until she got home. Then she never came back, and the power was out, and there was no school. So I saw all the people around your house and came over to watch your television debut."

"You saw that?"

"Guh… deh… huh," Charlie mumbled in her best impression of Andy. "Boy, I'm cold. Where did you get that jacket? It's too big for you. You look ridiculous. I'm soaked. All this rain. I think it's been raining since we moved here last week. We're from Seattle. My dad still lives there, but my parents aren't divorced. Does it always rain so much on this side of the mountains? I'll have to borrow some clothes."

Andy gave up trying to add to the conversation. He was also hungry, and wet, and knew he looked ridiculous in Mr. Hoffman's big coat, so he just nodded in agreement to Charlie's questions and led the way across Otter Lane and down the block to his house. He trudged around the crater to the porch, drawn forward by the food he knew was in the kitchen and the fireplace where he could make a fire. He was almost at the front door when he noticed Charlie was no longer at his side and no longer talking.

She was paralyzed at the sight of the dead alien lying at the bottom of the porch steps. She couldn't take her eyes off it. The creature's largest eye had yellowed and shriveled. The whole body seemed deflated, the brown fur matted and clumping. The rotting smell was like a punch in the nose. For the first time since leaving her house, Charlie was speechless.

"It's okay," Andy said. "It's dead."

"You sure? What if it's just sleeping."

"I don't think it's sleeping."

"How do you know? Have you seen an alien sleep before? Or die before? Maybe it's just hibernating. Maybe it'll wake up and shoot us with that thing."

She pointed to the weapon lying beside the alien. Andy returned to her side, took her arm, and led her past the body. "It's dead. I touched it before."

"You touched it?"

"It was in the way. C'mon."

He opened the front door, led her inside, then kicked the door closed. They walked down the hall, past the rain-soaked stairs, and into the kitchen. With the door closed and the darkness masking the debris in the back yard, the room looked almost normal as though at any moment his mom or dad would walk in and turn on the lights.

Andy found a flashlight in the junk drawer where batteries, light bulbs, and pizza delivery coupons were kept. He turned it on and set it on the counter so that the beam pointed straight up at the ceiling, filling the room with a soft light.

"I've never seen a dead thing before," Charlie said. "What are they? Where did they come from? What do they want?"

Andy waited for her to answer her own questions, but when she left them hanging, he shrugged, "I don't know."

He opened the refrigerator and grabbed a jar of lukewarm juice. He was tempted to drink right from the bottle, but fetched two glasses from the cupboard. They drank quietly, the silence filled with the sound of tapping rain and their own gulping.

Andy's plan had been to reach home, find a responsible adult, and do as they directed. He was very good at following directions. His life had depended on it. In the hospital, he ate whatever tasteless food the nurses gave him and went hungry when they said he must fast. He endured the treatments the doctor prescribed, despite how weak and nauseous they made him. He remained in bed the first month back home, not because he wanted to, but because he knew it's what his mom wanted and, more than that, what she needed. But now there was no one to follow, no one to tell him what to do.

"I'll be right back," Charlie said. "Don't go anywhere."

She took the flashlight and walked down the hall. Andy thought about following her, but heard the guest bathroom door close and decided against it. He wandered into the living room where everything was oddly normal. The knick-knacks his mother collected had fallen from the shelves by the fireplace, but every piece of furniture was still standing, though jostled out of place.

He knelt on the hearth, opened the fireplace screen, and set two large pieces of wood at either end of the grate. He filled the space between with crumpled newspaper on top of which he set kindling and another large piece of wood. He checked to make sure the flue was open, then used one of the matches kept on the mantle to light the wads of paper.

The fire crackled to life, spreading light and warmth across his face. He watched the flame burn across the paper and lap at the kindling that glowed red, then blackened as it was consumed. The flames spread like a living thing, embracing the larger pieces of wood until they too began to burn.

With the fire successfully launched, he walked to the front hall closet. There he found his red coat and an another jacket that would fit Charlie. A muffled noise drew his attention to the closed bathroom door.

He saw the glow at the base of the door and heard the sound of crying within. He thought about knocking or saying something comforting, but when he cried, the last thing he wanted was for anyone to notice. So he returned to the kitchen and gathered a loaf of bread, a pack of hotdogs, ketchup, relish, plates, another bottle of juice, and the giant fork his dad used to turn steaks on the barbecue. He returned to the living room, his arms full, and spread everything upon the hearth.

"Andy?" Charlie called in the kitchen. "Andy!"

"In here," he replied.

Charlie hurried into the room, eyes wide with panic. "Don't do that. Don't ever do that again!"

"Do what?"

"Leave me alone like that."

She knelt on the hearth. Her eyes were red, but wiped dry, and she smiled at the fire. "Nice work, but what if the aliens see the smoke? Won't they come back?"

"There's stuff burning all over the neighborhood," Andy replied. "I don't think one more fire will matter. Oh, I found you a jacket."

"Great. Dry clothes, fire, food. We rock! And I love hot dogs. Do you love hot dogs? I only put mustard on mine. That's something my dad taught me. Only have mustard on hot dogs. Never ketchup. Ketchup is for French fries. He lives in Seattle, but they aren't divorced. Or did I mention that already?"

Andy nodded as Charlie went on about the proper use of condiments. He speared two hot dogs onto the tines of the barbecue fork and held them over the fire. Things were going about as well as they possibly could under the circumstances. He had helped the new girl — saved her life, really — and found some degree of safety and comfort in his living room.

Even better, he didn't have to worry about making small talk. Charlie was holding up both ends of the conversation just fine, requiring only the occasional nod from Andy. Best of all, she had no idea he had ever been sick. He was just a normal kid to her. There was no pity or concern in her eyes, just a lively energy that made Andy forget about the whimpers he had heard through the bathroom door.

"How did you get out?" she asked. "I thought you were a goner. I saw that thing step through your house."

"My family made it to our truck and we took off. There was a traffic jam on the main road and my dad turned around and headed into the hills. The machine chased us — almost caught us too — but my folks made it into the tunnel on the Old Mill Road. I was thrown out the back. Landed in some bushes. Do you want to see all the cuts I got?"

"No thanks," she replied.

Andy was disappointed. Hector would want to see his cuts and scrapes and would certainly be impressed by their quantity and variety. He considered giving Charlie what his dad called the "nickel tour" of the house, but thought better of it. He was almost relieved his room had been destroyed. Something told him Charlie would not be impressed with the mess or his collection of models.

"I know that tunnel," Charlie said. "We drove through it when my mom showed me around the base. Have you been there before?"

"Once," Andy replied. "On a school tour. The whole class went. The base was built inside a mountain a long time ago when everyone was afraid of nuclear war. Now they just use it to talk with other bases built into other mountains. You said your mom works there?"

"She's in the army, like my dad, but she doesn't carry a rifle like he does. She works on computers. Oh, the hot dogs!"

In the fireplace, one hot dog had caught fire. Andy pulled out the big fork and blew on the flames. Charlie dealt slices of bread onto plates and spread mustard and relish over them. Both dogs were blackened, but it didn't matter. Folded into a slice of bread and slathered in mustard, they tasted great. They were the best hot dogs Andy had ever eaten. He started two more cooking while they ate. Charlie pinched her face into a serious expression.

"What do we do now?" she asked, her lips smudged with mustard.

There was that question again. What should they do now? Andy wanted to rest. The idea of sleep now consumed him as much as the idea of food had. He knew, however, that sleep is not the answer to Charlie's question. She looked at him, expecting something. It felt strange that someone looked to him for answers.

"My dad's an engineer and says that everything starts with a plan," he replied. "I think we should go to Pine Mountain. I think that's where my dad was heading. Makes sense. It would be the safest place in the valley."

"I thought you said the tunnel was blocked? How can we go there if the tunnel is blocked?"

"There's another road to it," Andy said, a plan taking shape in his mind. "The East Ridge Road, but I know a trail that's faster. I've hiked it before. It follows the Otter River up to Duck Lake. Yes, we should go to Pine Mountain. I'm sure that's where my family is. And your mom. And they'll have supplies and food. Armies have that sort of thing. We rest here tonight and leave in the morning."

They finished their meal and made a list of all the things they would need for the journey. Later, they dragged pillows off the couch and brought blankets from the closet to create makeshift beds on the floor before the fire.

That night, Andy dreamed of walking through a pounding rain, his feet cold and wet, his shirt soaked, and his hair plastered to his head. His parents walked just ahead, his mom carrying Freddie. Andy tried to catch up to them, but no matter how fast he walked, they only seemed to get farther away.

CHAPTER FOURTEEN

Trouble Returns

Andy jolted awake, a hand clamped over his mouth. His eyes shot open, then winced shut again, blinded by the morning light streaming through the living room windows.

Charlie knelt beside him, a finger pressed to her lips. Andy heard a crashing sound in the front yard. He thought of the tripod's probing tentacles and knew Charlie was thinking the exact same thing. It was all Andy could do to keep from yelling. Charlie pulled him behind the couch where they waited and listened.

"Touch it," someone outside said.

"I'm not gonna touch it," another voice replied.

"Don't be a wimp. Touch it."

"Get a stick."

"Poke its eye out."

"Gross."

"Sick, man. You are so sick!"

Andy recognized the voices and whispered, "Reggie."

"Who?" Charlie asked.

A window at the front of the room smashed, accompanied by a burst of laughter. Charlie shrieked. Andy clamped his hand over her mouth. Too late. The front door burst open, slamming into the wall. Ben Hickman and Lance Walker entered along with the stink of the cigarettes they smoked.

"I didn't hear anything," Ben said.

"I did," Lance replied. "We should burn this whole place down. That would be cool."

Andy stood up from behind the couch and yelled, "Hey! You're not burning my house down!"

Ben and Lance jumped. They were both wearing black, as usual. Andy wondered if their entire wardrobe was black, or if they just wore the same set of clothes every day. Their startled expressions turned to angry scowls as Reggie entered, a stick in one hand and cigarette in the other.

"What are you doing here, McBean?" he yelled, smoke leaking from his mouth as though his words were on fire.

"I live here. And my mom doesn't allow smoking in the house."

"Where are your parents?" Lance asked, suddenly wary.

"They're… sleeping upstairs," Andy lied.

"Let's go," Ben hissed.

Reggie dropped his cigarette on the floor and pressed it into the carpet with his boot. "No. He's lying. If his folks were here they'd have heard us. The Martian thing got them."

"They'll be back soon," Andy said. "And then you'll be in trouble."

"So they aren't here. I knew it," Reggie sneered. "They're dead. They're all dead. The machine got them just like it got Lori. Picked her up with those tentacles."

Charlie stood from behind the couch. "They're not dead!"

Ben and Lance jumped again. Even Reggie flinched.

"You? What're you doing here?"

"I was invited. You weren't," Charlie answered.

"We're going to the army base at Pine Mountain," Andy said. "We should be safe there."

"You're not going anywhere," Reggie shouted. "You owe me a fight."

"Kick his butt, Reggie," Lance goaded.

"Yeah, kick his butt," Ben laughed.

Spurred on by the others, Reggie crossed the living room and grabbed Andy by the collar.

"Hey!" Andy yelped.

"Stop it!" Charlie shouted.

Reggie ignored their pleas and dragged Andy out the front door to the cheers of Lance and Ben. He shoved Andy off the porch and past the dead alien at the bottom of the stairs. He stopped at a flat spot next to the mound of dirt around the alien ship and punched Andy without hesitation. Andy saw a flash of fist. His knees buckled and the ground rose up to meet his butt. He sat in the dirt, pain spreading across his chin.

"That's for hitting me with your trombone," Reggie said.

"Now just wait a sec…" Andy sputtered.

There was no waiting, not even for a second. Reggie grabbed Andy and hoisted him to his feet. The next punch slammed into Andy's cheek. He wobbled backward and Reggie's third blow caught nothing but air. Andy looked around for cover, but all he saw were the taunting faces of Ben and Lance.

"Go easy, Reg," Lance joked. "He may die again."

"Again?" Charlie asked.

"Don't you know who he is?" Reggie asked. "This is the kid who had…"

Andy dove at Reggie, throwing all his weight at him. The older boy was more surprised than hurt, as both landed on the dirt piled around the meteor. Andy knew it was a desperate move, but it succeeded in preventing Reggie from telling Charlie about his illness.

Now he would pay the price.

Reggie's next blow caught him square on the jaw. His face shuddered. Teeth rattled. Reggie pulled back for another punch. Andy braced for the pain. He crunched his eyes shut and waited, but the blow never came. Instead a loud crack split the air, startling everyone.

Andy opened his eyes and saw Reggie frozen mid-punch. The big eighth-grader stared toward the porch where Charlie stood, the dead alien's weapon in her hands. A tendril of green smoke rose from its glowing end.

"Leave him alone," she said coldly.

Andy had seen the dark look in Charlie's eyes before. He knew she meant business. Lance was the first to sense the situation had taken a dangerous turn and ran from the uncertainty as much the weapon in Charlie's hands. Ben turned to Reggie for guidance but didn't find any and ran after Lance. Reggie didn't move. He wasn't about to take orders from a sixth-grader. Andy held his breath, waiting to see who would blink first.

Charlie pointed the glowing weapon right at Reggie. "I'm not sure what this thing does, but I'm guessing it would hurt… a lot."

Reggie released Andy and looked around for a place to hide. He tripped over the melted blob that used to be a fire truck and fell to the pavement. As Charlie stepped closer, he scrambled to his feet and ran after his friends down the side yard of Andy's house. Even as his footsteps faded, Charlie aimed the weapon after him.

"Charlie? I think he's gone," Andy said.

She didn't lower the weapon and something in her focused eyes and tight mouth told Andy she wasn't about to.

"I knew that kid was a loser the moment I saw him in art class," she said.

"Charlie, I don't think that ray gun is a good idea."

"I wasn't gonna hurt them, Andy. Just scare them off."

"I think the aliens blast anything with a weapon. Like they did with the soldiers. Everyone else they put into those cages. You should get rid of it."

"We might need it."

"One weapon isn't going to hurt that tripod machine."

"Not for the machine," she replied. "For other things. For people. Bad people like those jerks."

"You hear something?"

"I wish my dad were here. He'd know what to do."

Andy cocked his head. "Charlie, I hear something."

"He lives in Seattle. I wish he were here now."

"Charlie, listen."

A puddle near Andy's feet rippled as the distant tremors grew louder. Each rumble sent dirt sliding down the crater wall. Someone yelled in the distance. A moment later, Reggie and Lance reappeared from around the house, Ben right behind them.

"Run!" Ben shouted, fear in his eyes.

CHAPTER FIFTEEN

Taken

Andy had almost forgotten about the alien tripod. With a belly full of hotdogs and a good night's sleep, he thought the worst was over. The thundering footfalls of the machine, however, brought the familiar terror back sharp and clear. He sat on the bank of the crater, paralyzed, his bruised face throbbing, and watched a puddle ripple with each tremor.

Charlie dropped the weapon and pulled Andy to his feet. "C'mon! Run!"

They ran up the street after the others as the armored helmet of the alien tripod rose into view behind Andy's home. The ground shook beneath them, making running difficult. Andy stole a glance over his shoulder and watched the machine step through what remained of the second floor of his house. Wood, bricks, and shingles flew into the street.

The machine quickly towered over them, blocking out the sun, its porthole glaring and silver tentacles reaching down. One glimpse of the slithering metal arms spurred Andy forward. Charlie faltered, stunned at the sight, but Andy caught her and pulled her on.

They easily passed the gasping Lance and red-faced Ben. The tripod was over the faltering boys in two thundering steps. One tentacle wrapped itself around Ben's waist, hoisting him into the air, his legs still pumping. Another knocked Lance to the ground and plucked him up by the legs.

Andy and Charlie ran on, cutting through the Garcia's yard and around the corner, passing Reggie who staggered and stumbled. Before he hit the pavement, however, a silver tentacle caught him and carried him into the air.

Hide, Andy thought. *Where can we hide?*

He knew the cars on the street offered little protection. Could they get into a house? His legs ached and his lungs burned. They couldn't run forever. He could see the exhaustion on Charlie's face. Straight ahead, a large storm drain was cut into a sidewalk curb. This was not a small drain with a metal grate, but a large person-sized opening designed to swallow the great torrents of water generated by winter storms and spring thaws.

"Charlie! The drain!" Andy yelled, pointing to it.

She was slowing, her face slack and dripping sweat. Andy ran to the drain and dove toward the opening. He scrambled and slid headfirst into the cement tunnel beneath the sidewalk, then reached back toward Charlie. She dove toward him. He grabbed her hands and pulled.

Something held her back.

"Don't let go," she gasped. "Don't let go."

They clutched at each other, but the tentacle holding her leg was too strong.

"Andy," she whispered.

And then she was gone.

Andy watched her dangling form rise toward the tripod. Another slithering appendage crossed the pavement toward him. On hands and knees, he backed into the dark reaches of the tunnel overcome with a pain he had never experienced before. It was far worse than the blows Reggie had inflicted on his face, the hunger in his stomach, or the ache in his legs from running. It was the pain of seeing Charlie yanked away, and the fear so keenly etched on her face.

The tentacle slid through the drain opening and fumbled blindly, its tapered end banging against the concrete walls. Andy crawled away from it, hands clutching at the slimy tunnel. The floor sloped down and he lost his grip, falling to his belly and sliding out of control. He tumbled and rolled down the shaft, thankful only that it took him far from the thrashing tentacle.

Then he fell.

And fell.

And fell some more.

Surrounded by darkness, he grabbed wildly at the air before splashing into a black pool. Water rushed into his open mouth. Struggling upward, he broke through the surface, gagging and coughing, and dog-paddled to keep his head above the water.

He couldn't see anything, but the sound of water echoing against hard walls told him he was in the holding tank for storm runoff. He was cold, wet, and sore, but away from the tentacles and that's what mattered. He thought the worst was over when familiar reverberations echoed in the chamber, quickly growing from loud to deafening. He clamped his hands over his ears to block out the tremors.

The sound grew so loud that he ducked under the frigid water. Looking up through the rippling surface, he watched cracks of light split the roof of the chamber. With a deafening crash, the ceiling collapsed and chunks of concrete splashed around him.

Light filled the holding tank. Andy saw another drain opening on a far wall. He splashed his way toward it as a tentacle descended through the broken ceiling, feeling blindly about tank. Two more tentacles squirmed their way through the opening, fumbling along the walls and splashing through the water. One passed right over Andy's head.

He sucked in a deep breath and swam underwater as another tentacle reached toward him. At the mouth of the exit drain, he lifted his body out of the pond. He didn't need any encouragement to slide down the tunnel, but plenty was provided as a tentacle brushed across his foot. With remarkable dexterity, the mechanical snake grabbed hold of him.

Andy jerked his foot away, but the tentacle held tight.

Desperate, he tugged the velcro straps on his shoe loose and pulled his foot free, then slid once more into darkness.

Tumbling and turning, he wrapped his arms around his head to protect his face. Far ahead, a light appeared and grew closer with each tumble. Andy fell out of the storm drain, landing with a splat on the muddy banks of Otter Creek. He sat there a moment, cold and shivering, and made a mental note to wear his skateboard helmet the next time he fled from alien war machines.

Rolling onto his knees, he coughed up the last gulps of water from his lungs, then struggled to his feet. His pants and shirt were torn and his head ached. He touched the pain and drew away dabs of blood. But he was alive, and no tentacles emerged from the drain pipe to grab him.

He stood and limped along the edge of the bank until he found the trail back to the neighborhood. He stayed to the bushes. Down the street the tripod remained over the holding pond, its tentacles reaching into the hole they had created. Strange plumes of vapor drifted out of the pit.

Charlie.

She stood along with Reggie and the others beside the machine. An alien aimed a weapon right at them.

No.

On the pavement near them was an empty cage with spinning bars of light. Another alien manipulated a small device just like the one Andy had seen by the dead alien on his front porch. The breeze carried a strange melody to his ears.

The cage bars stopped spinning and parted wide enough for Charlie and the others to be pushed inside. Andy heard the melody again as the bars closed. The tripod crouched over the cage and when it stood again the cage came with it, attached to its belly.

The machine stood to its full height, turned to the left and the right, then marched down the main road toward West Bend. Andy waited until it was well out of sight before leaving his hiding place. He limped toward the hole the tentacles had punched into the storm basin. The concrete chamber was empty. Not only empty, but bone dry.

Dazed and shaken, Andy walked up Otter Lane to what remained of his house, limping past wrecked cars, destroyed homes, and the great ditch the alien ship had carved on its way to his front yard. He thought about Charlie, trapped in the alien cage with Reggie, Ben, and Lance. They would all be scared and frightened, but Charlie most of all. She was new and had no friends here.

Andy walked past the meteor shell and the dead alien, barely giving either a second glance. He walked through the front door, which refused to close properly, and back to the living room. The couch pillows were on the floor where he and Charlie had spent the night by the fireplace. He thought about making a fire again, but could only slump onto the pillows, exhausted. He assumed he would cry — crying made perfect sense in this situation — but for some odd reason no tears came.

Instead, he felt angry, the same anger that drove his trombone into Reggie's gut. He clenched his fist, eager to find something to ram or smash, then remembered his dad's advice about channeling his feelings in a more constructive direction. A strange idea took hold of him, one that made absolutely no sense and was almost certain to fail.

He went to the bathroom, washed his face, and bandaged his scrapes and cuts. He found a fresh change of clothes in the laundry room and laced up his hiking boots over a bright pair of clean socks.

From the front closet, he found his school backpack and dumped out the textbooks, note pads, pencils, and pens. He replaced them with food, water, a flashlight, binoculars, first aid kit, and a box of matches. Then he bundled himself in his familiar red jacket and baseball cap and swung the backpack onto his shoulders.

He left through the front door and didn't even bother to close it. Stepping off the porch he stopped by the dead alien and picked up the device laying beside it. It was about the size of a football and topped with a large knob. He brushed the mud off it and turned the knob. Soft musical tones played.

Andy smiled, certain it was the same type of device used to open and close the alien cage. He shoved it into his pack and retraced his steps to the entrance of his neighborhood. There he stood amidst the empty cars and looked up the hill toward the Old Mill Road. He could take the road to the trail that followed the Otter River to Duck Lake. It passed around the blocked tunnel and on to the Pine Mountain Army Base. He knew his parents and Freddie were there. He felt it. If he started now he could make the base by nightfall.

That had been the plan.

But plans change.

Andy set off in the opposite direction, down the road pocked with tripod footprints toward West Bend, determined to set his new friend free.

Been'Tok cowered under Gorn'Mek's wrath. As operator of the Grabbers, he should have captured the Great Warrior in his watery lair, but for all his efforts, he only retrieved a shoe.

The Warrior had evaded capture again.

The four bipeds they had caught were meager consolation, and only the discovery of the underground pool softened Gorn'Mek's rage. He ordered Been'Tok to use the Grabbers and suck up every drop of water while the new captives were placed in a pen.

By the time they had finished, Been'Tok's projector sparked to life. Tarak'Nor's holographic face appeared over him and barked new orders. The Seeker crew would search the nearby village on foot. They had filled several pens with bipeds, but more creatures could be hiding inside the structures and the Warrior may be among them.

Been'Tok shuddered at the prospect. It would mean leaving the Seeker. His harness would filter the air, but the planet's unusual gravity made it difficult to walk. Field duty had never been his strongest skill.

He envied the Masters who rested comfortably in their gravity-controlled ship. They didn't go on patrols, conduct searches, or do any of the difficult things that Workers had to do. As the Seeker marched back to the biped hive, Been'Tok was filled with the *feeling-that-needed-a-name*. Orders are orders, however, and he dutifully crawled out of the Grabber turret and prepared for the exit ramp to open.

CHAPTER SIXTEEN

The Mission

Andy approached downtown West Bend by the river trail, keeping to the cover of trees and bushes. It felt good to wear a fresh change of clothes, sturdy hiking boots, and his familiar red jacket. The backpack around his shoulders swayed with every step, the alien device inside clinking against the canteen of water.

When the trail opened at Founders Park, he could see the alien machine standing over Main Street between Reeseman's Drug Store and Henderson Hardware. The body of the tripod was even taller than the steeple of the Methodist Church.

Andy crept through the park, past picnic tables, playground equipment, and the bronze statue of Ezra Taggert, founder of West Bend. He could not count the number of times his family had picnicked here on warm summer days, his mom dishing up potato salad and his dad barbecuing salmon while Andy and Freddie swam. He wondered if he would ever enjoy such days again.

He shook the memories from his mind as another sound joined the gentle current of the Otter River; the cries and shouts of people. Andy headed toward the noise, running to the back side of the B-Liner Diner. Between it and the neighboring Post Office was a narrow space less than a meter wide. He slipped down the gap to the far end where he could see all of Main Street.

He hardly recognized his town.

Cars filled the street, turned every which way, some crushed by the feet of the alien tripod. Garbage and debris drifted on the wind. The front wall of the Lucky Nite Tavern had been completely destroyed. Even the corner of West Bend Savings and Loan, with its stately columns, had been smashed. For all the devastation, what he didn't see was even sadder.

There were no people.

Sidewalks normally filled with shoppers were barren and shop doors swayed open and closed as though used by ghosts. He had never seen his town so empty and hollow, like a toy town in a giant train set.

Down the street, the tripod stood at the intersection of Main and Taggert. Crouching low on bending legs, it set the glowing cage holding his friends beside two other cages, each crowded with people. Their cries and moans drifted down the street to the shadows where he hid. He wanted to shield his ears from the noise, but forced himself to listen.

He was on a mission.

He tugged the backpack off his shoulders and pulled the alien device from it. Holding it before him, he twisted the top just as he had seen the alien do. Gentle musical notes played, but nothing happened. The weaving bars of light that defined each cage continued to rotate. He turned the knob again, but the cages did not open. Perhaps he wasn't close enough.

The tripod hissed and groaned, releasing a cloud of vapor. A panel beside the porthole snapped open and a ramp unfolded to the street. Brown figures ambled out of the cabin. Andy ducked back into the shadows.

He returned the round device to his backpack and pulled out the binoculars his dad used for hunting. Through them he could see the aliens clearly. Each creature wore a metal device around its shoulders and carried a weapon like the one Charlie had used to scare off Reggie. Five waddled down the ramp, gliding more than walking on three legs. Their fur ranged from dark brown to rusty tan and reminded him of the brown bears in the Port Cascade Zoo. Four were not much taller than himself, one even shorter, but the fifth was much bigger. A giant. The scowl on its face and the way it barked at the others reminded Andy of Reggie.

Even aliens have thugs, Andy thought.

A cloud of light materialized before the Thug alien. Andy watched the cloud form into a giant alien face. Its head was even larger than the Thug's, and it bellowed strange words in a deep voice.

Big Heads, Andy thought. *They must be the alien leaders.*

The floating hologram of the Big Head faded. The Thug barked to the smaller aliens, who spread out to either side of the street, their weapons at the ready.

Andy put the binoculars away and retreated down the narrow alley. He stayed close to the adjoining buildings, working his way past Wanda's Beauty Parlor and the West Bend Medical Clinic, where Doctor Kline gave him and Freddie their yearly check-ups. Finally, he stood at the back of the West Bend Professional Building where his father worked on the second floor.

He had visited the Olympic Construction Company many times and knew the front windows looked down on Main Street and might be close enough to open the alien cages. Best of all, Andy knew the combination for the lock on the back door.

The staircase at the back of the building took him to the second floor landing where he punched the code on the door lock. It clicked and he snuck inside. Only when he closed the door behind him did he breathe a sigh of relief.

The office was empty and dark. Straight ahead, stairs led down to the flower shop on the first floor. Off to the right were desks stacked with the drawings used to build houses and buildings. Andy crept past them, wincing at every creak his footsteps made. The closer he got to the front windows, the lower he crouched, until finally he crawled across the floor to the wall beneath one window.

Peering through the venetian blinds, he could see one large tripod leg. The metal was shiny in some parts and a dull gray in others. Each joint was a large knuckle like the knees on the skeleton in Mr. Sandoval's biology class.

He dared to part the blinds enough to look onto the street below where the glowing cages sat in the middle of the intersection. Green bands of light arced around them in random directions, like a woven basket.

A jingling noise from the first floor drifted up the stairs. Andy caught his breath. Something had opened the door to the flower shop, and judging from its strange barking voice, it wasn't human.

CHAPTER SEVENTEEN

A Close Encounter

The alien crashed and banged through the flower shop downstairs. Andy crawled to his father's desk. Just kneeling beside it was comforting. In one corner, near the phone and stapler, was a framed photo of Andy in his muddy soccer uniform. He remembered the day it was taken. How could he forget?

It was the day the West Bend Otters defeated their arch rivals the Port Warden Badgers. It was also the day he received the bruise to his shin while scoring the equalizer. A week later, his leg remained so blue and yellow that his mom took him to Doctor Kline, who sent them to Doctor Hilyard in Port Cascade for tests. It was the last day he had been healthy. The day he learned a bruise that doesn't heal is one symptom of leukemia.

Footsteps creaked up the stairs. Andy ducked into the alcove of the desk and pressed his face to the floor. Through the gap at the bottom of the desk he watched the grunting alien reach the top of the stairs. It was the largest one, the Thug. The creature lumbered across the office, pausing at the snack table to inspect the industrial coffee maker. With an angry bark, it swept its weapon across the table, scattering packets of sugar and containers of cream.

"Psst."

Andy cocked his head at the sound. It had come from behind him, but perhaps it had just been his blinky hearing. He returned his attention to the alien stalking through the office.

"Psst."

There it was again. Behind him were other desks and behind them a wall filled with construction drawings. Nothing seemed out of place.

"Psst."

Andy followed the sound to the base of the desk behind him. Just above the floor, two green eyes stared out. Someone was hiding under that desk just like he was. The eyes kept looking toward the stairs. Did the person think Andy should run for it? Were they crazy? He would be caught for sure.

Andy shook his head, rejecting the idea. A hand joined the eyes and pointed to the stairs, then made an arcing motion as though throwing something. That's it. Throw something down the stairs to distract the alien. There was no way the person could throw something from his or her position, but Andy could.

He nodded, but a terrible smell drew his attention to the crack beneath the desk. There, just inches away, stood the alien's large feet with wide toenails in serious need of clipping. Andy held his breath until the alien wandered off again, its attention drawn to the supply closet across the room.

He reached out of the alcove to the top of the desk and felt for something to throw. His fingers found a soft rubber ball. It was one of those stress balls grown-ups use to remind them how happy they were as kids when they didn't have to work and could go outside and play.

He glanced to the other desk. The green eyes were still there, the hand pointing to the stairs. Andy nodded, took a deep breath, then tossed the rubber ball over the stair railing. It fell down the stairs, bouncing noisily from step to step.

The Thug alien hurried toward the sound to investigate. It barked and jabbered, its weapon raised, then clomped back down the stairs. As the tip of its strange head disappeared, someone pulled Andy from the alcove.

"Let's go," whispered a woman with green eyes.

She led him across the office to the supply closet and pulled the door open. Andy recognized her as a coworker of his father's, but could not remember her name. She was the first grown-up he'd seen since falling out the back of the family pickup and there were many things to ask her. What were these creatures? Where had they come from? What did they want? Could she help him open the cages in the street below? Did she know what happened to his parents and brother? Can she help find them?

"Get in," she said, then closed the closet door behind her. "You're Martin's son. What are you doing here? Never mind. We can't stay here. Those things will come back."

Before Andy could ask even one question or show her the device in his backpack, the woman pulled a short length of rope that dangled from the ceiling. A trapdoor swung down revealing a hatch. A ladder unfolded and she stepped upon it and opened the hatch. Blinding daylight flooded in. Satisfied the coast was clear, she motioned for Andy to climb up through the hatch.

He didn't have to be told twice. The grunts of the Thug had returned to the office outside the closet. Andy climbed through the hatch onto the tar-paper roof of the building. Vents, pipes, and metal boxes of mechanical equipment rose here and there. A low brick wall framed the roof and he crawled to it, expecting the woman to join him, but she simply pulled the hatch closed. He heard the creaking ladder folding back in place.

Then a door burst open.

A muffled shriek.

A burst of alien shouts.

Then silence.

Andy hugged his backpack to his chest and wrapped his arms around it. Why hadn't the woman followed him? Maybe his entire plan was a mistake? Had he been foolish to think he could free Charlie and the other captives? The

*The familiar door jingle drew his attention over the side of the
building where the alien machine crouched on the street.*

jingle of the door drew his attention over the side of the building where the alien machine crouched on the street. He could see a cage beside it, and recognized Mrs. Holland, the owner of the Rialto Theater, Mr. Massari, who worked at the B-Liner Diner, and many others from the town.

The big alien pushed the woman out of the flower shop and to the cage. She stole a glance over her shoulder to the top of the building where Andy hid. The thumbs-up sign she made, however, gave him little comfort. A smaller alien approached with a round device just like the one in Andy's backpack. It turned the knob back and forth, musical notes played, and the bars of the cage parted. The Thug shoved the woman with green eyes inside.

The smaller alien worked the device again, producing a different melody. The cage closed. The cries and whimpers of the captives were too much for Andy to bear. He clamped his hands over his ears. They muffled the sound of misery below, but could not block the scream of the cannon shell that soared over the town and exploded on the southern ridge.

CHAPTER EIGHTEEN

The Battle of West Bend

The first artillery shell exploded on the southern ridge, setting several trees ablaze. Andy crouched beneath the parapet as a second projectile screamed through the sky. There was no green blast of energy. This was something different. It was the army.

A third shell thundered overhead. Andy ducked for cover as the explosion echoed across the valley. He looked north and saw a puff of white smoke on a high ridge. Another appeared even before the first had dissipated. The blast of the cannon arrived a moment later, followed by the screaming shell and another explosion to the south. A fiery spruce toppled in a thundering crash of branches, taking many smaller trees with it.

Andy peered over the brick wall just enough to watch aliens scramble out of various buildings and stare at the sky, their strange eyes blinking. The holographic face of the Big Head appeared over each of them, barking orders.

The aliens ambled back to the tripod as fast as their stubby legs would carry them. Andy lost sight of them under the crouching body of the machine, but moments later, the tripod rose on straightened legs. He ducked behind the wall. With one sweeping stride, the tripod stepped over the building, one foot landing in the back alley with a crunching thud. Andy pressed himself flat on his back, awestruck as the body of the machine moved over him, its tentacles swaying back and forth.

The tripod stomped through Founder's Park, knocking the statue of Ezra Taggert from its pedestal, and crossed the Otter River in one step. Its tremors diminished with distance, replaced by the sounds of shouting and crying from the cages it had left behind on the street.

Andy thought of the woman who had sacrificed herself to save him. This was his chance. With the aliens distracted, he could open the cages and set the captives free. He crawled to the trap door, lifted it open, and pressed his feet upon the hatch. The ladder unfolded to the floor of the supply closet and he climbed down.

He opened the closet door and found the office empty and quiet save for the faint shudders of the departing tripod. He walked to the stairs and started down. Every creak filled him with fear, but soon he was at the bottom of the stairs, surrounded by brightly colored flowers.

Out the flower shop's windows he could see the cages of people. He walked toward the front door and a burst of staccato barks and clicks outside drew his attention. An alien ambled across the street toward him.

It was a smaller creature, perhaps the smallest of the bunch, but carried a weapon all the same. Andy ducked for cover behind a stand of large sunflowers, hoping the alien hadn't seen him. The familiar jingle of the shop door opening proved him wrong.

Peering through the flowers, he watched the shuffling alien enter. The way its feet flopped reminded him of a clown in ridiculously large shoes. Its body was pear-shaped, with the head taking up the smaller end. He didn't know if it was a boy alien or a girl alien, or if aliens even had boys and girls. Aside from the weapon it carried, the alien wore only the metal device around its shoulders.

Vents on the device clicked open and closed as the creature moved from one floral display to the next. There was something gentle in its three eyes, heavy lids blinking, as they looked from flower to flower. Its wide fingers delicately stroked each blossom and lifted them for closer inspection. Gasps of delight escaped the creature's mouth, reminding Andy of Mr. Anders' dog Bucky chewing on its favorite toy. He was almost certain they were gasps of pleasure.

Perhaps these aliens were not as fierce as he had imagined. He had never considered that beings who controlled such terrifying machines would also marvel at the beauty of a daffodil or a carnation. Maybe there was nothing on their world as pretty as a rose.

The alien stepping closer. Before Andy could react, the creature picked up the large sunflower that hid his face. Andy was so stunned he could not move, not even to scream. Then the alien's mouth opened, revealing wide flat teeth. It shrieked. Andy decided this would be a good time to scream, so he did.

Both shouted until they were out of breath, then they filled their lungs to scream more. The alien stumbled backward, tripping and falling into a stand of tulips. Shelves crashed, dumping pots and plants onto its head. It dropped its weapon and the green tip glowed bright then exploded in a brilliant flash.

Every flower in the shop burst into a cloud of petals that swirled in the air like a rainbow. Red, blue, magenta, and yellow settled over the floor and onto the fallen alien like drops of paint.

Andy ran to the front door and threw it open, but something stopped him. It was a sound, or more accurately the absence of a sound. The steady clicking of the alien's breathing apparatus had stopped. Every bone in Andy's body wanted to run, but a choking noise drew him back to the alien, who lay motionless on the floor.

Andy saw the problem at once. The vent on the creature's metal shawl was jammed shut by a shard of pottery. The alien's mouth opened and closed like a fish out of water, lips pale and eyes dull, all three of them looking at Andy through fluttering lids.

Andy kneeled by the creature. Why should he care if this alien could not breathe? They had wrecked Otter Lane, ruined his mom's rose garden, destroyed his bedroom, and trapped half the town in cages. Why should he care?

With a final gasp, the alien fell still and silent.

Been'Tok slipped to death. He couldn't breathe. His respirator was malfunctioning and he lacked the strength to fix it. He took some comfort that his last sight was a dancing swirl of flower petals floating around him. He would very much like to touch them and add them to his collection, but his collecting days were over.

He should have followed orders.

Gorn'Mek commanded him to guard the captured bipeds while the rest of the Seeker crew destroyed the weapons firing wildly at them. Those were his orders and he was a Worker and Workers always obeyed Guardians. His attempt to calm the bipeds, however, had failed miserably. His smile resulted in gasps and screams. Several captives hid their faces. One jettisoned a volume of liquid from its mouth.

Discouraged, he turned his attention to the plant-filled building across the street. The prospect of studying so many growing things in one location was irresistible. Entering the room, he could barely contain himself. Each new blossom was a marvel of shape and color. He held flower after flower, delighting in their variety. But it had all been a trick.

The Great Warrior appeared from behind a large flower and attacked with a piercing scream. The rest was a blur of colors, first the green blast of his weapon, then the swirl of floating petals, and finally a growing darkness.

The end was near. Been'Tok did not fear death, but regretted the waste his life had been. The mind-numbing labor under the harsh demands of the Masters had kept him from learning all the things he wanted to know, but hadn't been taught.

As darkness closed, the Warrior stood victoriously over him and he wondered if his image would join the other vanquished foes on the biped's ceremonial robes.

CHAPTER NINETEEN

Rescue

Andy kneeled on the petal-covered floor and stared at the pale, lifeless alien. Its large eyes had the same vacant look as the dead one sprawled across the steps of his front porch, but this was different. The alien by his house had been killed by a soldier's bullet, while Andy had let this one die.

His parents always told him that actions have consequences, but sometimes doing nothing can be even worse. He reached down and took hold of the pottery shard stuck in the alien's respirator vent. It was jammed tight. He braced his legs and put his back to the task. The shard broke free sending him falling on his rump.

He watched the alien, looking for any sign of life. The respirator clicking open and closed. Once. Twice.

The alien gasped!

"Hah!" Andy shouted.

His sense of accomplishment turned to concern as the

alien blinked, eyes focusing, and the color returned to its lips. Andy rolled to his feet and ran out of the store.

On the sidewalk outside, he ducked as another mortar shell screamed overhead and exploded on the southern ridge. He looked north and saw the alien tripod amongst the trees, climbing toward the army cannons, its weapon glowing green.

Whoever is firing that cannon better run, Andy thought, *or improve their aim fast.*

"Get out of here!" someone yelled.

"Run!"

The voices came from the nearest cage. Panicked faces stared at him through glowing bars. He recognized Mr. Toland, vice-principal at West Bend Elementary, and Doc Stevens who owned the Car Doctor Body Shop. They continued to shout at him as he slung off his backpack. Andy wanted to explain he was here to help, but they shooed him away. He was, after all, *cancer boy*. How could he possibly help them?

He pulled the alien device from his pack and held it high. "I can get you out!" he shouted. "I can open the cages."

Everyone recognized the alien contraption. As another cannon shell rocketed overhead, Andy approached the cage, holding the device before him. He twisted the knob and the melodic notes played. The cage hummed alive, but instead of opening, the bars of light cinched tighter, squeezing everyone closer together.

"Stop!" Mr. Toland yelled. "Turn it the other way!"

Andy twisted the device in the opposite direction, producing a different series of notes, but the cage kept shrinking, squeezing the captives. He blocked out their cries and tried to remember how the alien used the device. It was a kind of musical combination lock. Andy's knew about music, tempo, and rhythm from his years playing the trombone, and with a calming breath, he turned the knob to play the same melody the aliens used to open the cage.

The bars instantly stopped tightening and reversed direction. The prisoners sighed in relief, then cheered as the bars spread wide enough apart to create openings big enough to stumble through. They ran from the cage, gasping for breath. No one stopped to thank Andy. They were all drawn to a new sound that joined the din of cannon fire, explosions, and shouting. A convoy of army trucks rumbled across the Otter River Bridge and right down Main Street.

"Look," a woman shouted. "The army!"

She ran to the trucks and many followed her, shouting and waving. Some people ran so fast they knocked others to the pavement. Andy stood his ground like a boulder in a river of people, looking for his friends in the rushing tide.

"Andy!" someone called from the next cage.

He ran to the second cage that was filled with expectant faces, and found one belonging to his friend. "Hector!"

"Dude, you're alive!" Hector shouted. "I thought you were toast for sure."

"We got away in the pick-up. I saw your mom's minivan."

"We tried to get out, but got stuck in that jam, then that thing came back and..."

"Hey!" someone interrupted. "Open the cage already!"

"Oh, right. Stand back," Andy said confidently.

This time he knew just what to do, and twisted the knob to play the melody perfectly. The light-bars spread open and those inside surged out, running right past Andy.

"You're welcome," he said. "My pleasure. Don't mention it. Really it was nothing."

"What happened to you?" Hector asked. "Where are your folks?"

"We drove into the hills. Made it to the tunnel on the Old Mill Road before that thing shot us."

"Shot you?"

"Yeah. My folks got away, but I fell out of the truck."

"Andy!" someone yelled.

"Charlie!"

"Charlie?" Hector asked. "Who's Charlie?"

Andy rushed to the to the last cage, Hector right behind him. Charlie stood on the other side of the bars, arms folded, eyes glaring.

"Any time this week," she said.

"Okay, okay," Andy replied. "Keep your pants on."

"You're Charlie?" Hector asked.

"Charlie, this is Hector," Andy said. "Hector, Charlie."

Andy played the melody again and the bars unfurled.

People tumbled out, among them the woman from his dad's office. She gave Andy a quick hug then ran with the crowd toward the army trucks. She was gone before he could ask her name.

Charlie approached, dirty and exhausted. Andy braced himself for a pat on the back, or a two-handed handshake, maybe even a hug. Probably a hug. Charlie seemed like the hugging type. After all, he had just rescued her and half the town. Definitely a hug.

She punched him in the arm. "Bout time. I thought I was gonna be stuck in there with Reggie forever."

Ben and Lance ran out of the cage without a word, but Reggie jumped through the bars with a growl. He stepped right up to Andy, face smeared with grime and sweat, eyes blazing with fear and anger. Andy backed up a step, bracing himself for a blow.

The big eighth-grader hugged him.

"Thank you," Reggie gushed. "Thank you."

Reggie leaned all his weight on Andy's shoulders, holding him tight, and heaved sobs of relief.

"Thank you. Thank you."

"Jeez, Reggie."

"Thank you."

"Okay, you're welcome already."

"Thank you."

Another mortar screamed overhead. Reggie yelped and let go of Andy. He ran toward the army trucks, shouting

"Thank you," over and over. Charlie and Hector watched the cannon shell explode on the southern ridge, shattering more trees.

"What are they doing?" Charlie asked. "They're way off target."

"Weekend warriors," Hector groaned. "Couldn't hit the broad side of a barn from the inside."

Andy looked north where the tripod approached the latest puff of cannon smoke. The tripod's weapon glowed bright green. He turned away, unwilling to watch the devastation he knew was coming.

Then another puff of smoke bloomed to the east. The boom of the cannon blast reached the town just as the shell slammed into the alien machine. The tripod staggered on its spindly legs, engulfed in smoke and flame. Everyone on Main Street gasped. Some shouted in surprise, others cheered.

"It was a decoy," shouted Andy. "A diversion to lure the machine out of town."

It was all clear now; the cannon to the north had never intended to hit the tripod when it stood in town with people nearby. Instead, the army had fired harmlessly at the southern ridge to lure the aliens out of West Bend and into a devastating cross fire.

When the tripod turned east to the source of the latest blast, another cannon fired from west, knocking it forward. When the machine turned west, the cannon to the east blasted it again, rocking the machine and sending the green rays it fired into a grove of fir trees. No matter which way the machine turned, a cannon shell slammed into its blind side. There was only one avenue of retreat. The tripod ran at full stride back toward West Bend.

"Andy," Charlie yelled. "Let's go!"

She ran toward the convoy of trucks, Hector right on her heels. Andy ran after them, but the street shook as the tripod approached. The tremors shattered windows and crumbled walls. A woman screamed and pointed at something over the Lucky Nite Tavern. The tripod loomed above the building, its hull shrouded in smoke, fire licking its dented armor as though it had just escaped from hell.

"Andy!" another voice yelled over the din.

He searched the crowd of fleeing people, but could not see who had called his name. He knew the voice. He knew it almost as well as his own.

"Andy!" the voice called again.

"Dad!"

CHAPTER TWENTY

Reunion

A ndy searched the fleeing crowd for his dad and spotted him down the street, standing in front of Annie's Craft Emporium.

"Dad!" he screamed.

His dad looked right at him and waved. Andy was so relieved at the sight that he barely flinched when the tripod stepped over the Rialto Theater, knocking its neon sign to the sidewalk. Hector yelped. Charlie pulled him to hide behind the sign as the alien machine straddled Main Street. She yelled for Andy to follow, but a cannon shell thundered into the tripod, drowning out her voice.

A blast of hot air knocked Andy to the pavement. Metal groaned and squealed as the tripod staggered like an old man, one leg breaking in a burst of sparks. The body stumbled upon its severed leg, the two remaining limbs clutching at the pavement, trying to compensate. The effort was futile and the tripod teetered, falling right toward Andy.

He was frozen with fear, unable to move as sparks rained all around him. The din of battle and screaming voices faded. All he could see and hear was the flaming body of the alien machine falling at him.

Someone pulled him out of the way at the last moment. Everything went black as he was thrown to the hard pavement. He heard a deafening crash and felt the earth ripple. The impact threw everything — people, cars, trash, everything — into the air.

Then silence.

Andy couldn't hear anything but a steady ringing. He opened his eyes and shook his head, but the sound would not stop. Straight ahead, the alien machine lay on its side forming a wall from one side of Main Street to the other. Andy knew his dad was on the other side of the broken tripod, but saw no way around or over the mass of twisted legs and limp tentacles.

Someone grabbed him and rolled him onto his back. He stared up at a furry face with three large eyes. It was the alien from the flower shop. Flower petals still littered its fur. Andy gasped and tried to crawl away, but the creature held him tight. Its lips moved, and though Andy couldn't hear what it said, there was something disarming about its expression.

The alien pulled him to his feet and dragged him toward the movie theater. They ducked behind the fallen neon sign. The alien pointed to the tripod where a hatch burst open in a blast of sparks. Figures stumbled out, the Thug alien first, followed by three others, all carrying weapons. The Thug fired green bolts, setting a storefront ablaze. The others opened fire with their own weapons, blasting windows and turning abandoned cars into a melting blobs.

Andy gasped at the sight.

The Thug turned to the sound.

The small alien beside Andy pulled him into the theater as the neon sign behind them glowed and slumped into a molten mass. Andy searched the dark lobby for his friends. He knew the candy counter was off to the right and hurried in that direction, the alien right behind him. Ducking behind it, they were greeted by twin gasps from Hector and Charlie, who cowered beneath the soda machine.

Andy crouched beside them and nodded toward the alien. "It's okay. He's with me."

The lobby doors burst open. Through the glass display case, Andy watched the Thug enter the lobby, its weapon at the ready. Hector squeaked. Andy and Charlie both clamped hands over his mouth. The big alien approached the counter and drove its weapon into the display case, shattering the glass. It grabbed a fistful of liquorice ropes and shoved them whole into its mouth.

The room shuddered. Condiment bottles and napkin holders toppled off the counter. Soda pop cups and paper bags fell on Andy's head. The door to the popcorn machine opened, releasing an avalanche of yellow kernels onto the alien beside him. The Thug barked and backed out of the theater. As the doors closed behind him, Andy peaked over the edge of the wrecked counter.

"Where'd it go?" Charlie asked.

"Who cares?" Hector replied. "As long as it's gone. But why isn't this one going too?"

"Let's take a look," Andy said.

They crept to the front of the lobby and looked through the windows. The aliens on the street were bathed in green light from above. Metal tentacles, much larger than those of the wrecked tripod, descended from the sky. Their tapered ends wrapped around the aliens and lifted them into the air. The large Thug was the last to go, and fired parting blasts into the building across the street.

"It's their big ship," Hector whispered. "It came this morning to pick up other cages of people. My mom and dad were in one of them."

"Where did it take them?" Andy asked.

"I don't know. We just saw lights above the clouds. They headed west toward Port Cascade."

The lobby rattled. Tendrils of dust drifted from the ceiling where cracks spidered across the plaster. Andy pushed the door open and stepped behind the melted remains of the theater sign. The aliens were gone, but Main Street was still bathed in greenish light. Andy brushed dust and dirt from his jacket. The small alien shook itself from head to toe, like a wet dog, then uttered a series of barks and clicks.

The words were incomprehensible, but at least Andy could hear them. The ringing in his ears had faded, replaced by the whine of the ship overhead, and the sound of destruction around them. A beam of green light split the clouds and struck the fallen tripod, setting it ablaze. The alien hurried down the street, paused to look back, then continued on. Charlie and Hector followed, but Andy looked toward the burning tripod, knowing his dad was somewhere on the other side.

"Andy!" someone called.

A figure stood amidst the smoke and flames.

"Dad!" Andy yelled.

He ran down the burning street, through flame and smoke and the blinding green ray beams. He ran to his dad's outstretched arms, buried his face into Martin's chest, and breathed the welcome scent of sweat and aftershave.

"Andy," Martin cried. "I found you."

"Where's Mom?" Andy asked.

"She's safe."

"And Freddie?"

"He's safe too. I'll take you to them."

CHAPTER TWENTY-ONE

Bacon

Andy and his dad ran from the burning street to the cover of the forest at the western end of town. There they found Charlie and Hector and climbed a gentle slope, not stopping until they collapsed upon a grassy clearing. Gasping for breath, Andy sprawled across his dad, reassured at the rise and fall of his chest.

The worst was over. His crazy plan had worked better than hoped and now his dad was here. They would go to Pine Mountain and see his Mom and brother. He would have plenty to eat and a bed to sleep in. The army would destroy the alien invaders and everyone would start to rebuild the homes, buildings, and streets the terrible machine had destroyed. It would take time, maybe months, but things would eventually return to normal.

For several minutes they caught their breath and watched the fiery destruction of West Bend. Eventually, the machine above the clouds stopped firing green rays and soared right over them, vanishing beyond the ridge.

Martin stood and helped everyone to their feet. "Don't worry. The army got the survivors out of town before that big ship arrived."

"But you stayed," Andy said.

"'Course I did," Martin replied, holding Andy close.

Andy looked around for the alien that had saved his life. "Hey, what happened to… it?"

Charlie shrugged her shoulders. Hector did the same.

"What happened to what, son?"

"It was one of them, Dad. One of the aliens. He… it… pulled me out of the way when the tripod fell."

"One of those things helped you?"

"Yes, it saved me."

"Maybe it was picked up like the others," Charlie offered.

"Maybe. Dad, this is Charlie. Charlie, my dad."

"Pleasure to meet you, Charlie," Martin said, then added with a glance to the setting sun. "It will be dark soon. We should get going."

Martin started up the hill, Andy beside him. He didn't know where his dad intended to go, but was only too happy to follow. He had made enough decisions for one week, and the weariness tugged at him. He was so tired that he could hardly keep his head up. His legs ached and his arms swayed limp. He looked at Hector and knew he was just as exhausted, but Charlie seemed fine.

"You look a lot like Andy," she said to Martin. "You have the same hair. I have my mom's hair, but my dad's eyes. We just moved here from Seattle. My dad still lives there, but they aren't divorced. My mom works at Pine Mountain. That's where Andy and I were going before the alien machine caught me."

Hector nudged Andy and whispered, "Does she always talk this much?"

"I'm afraid so," Andy replied.

They walked across the hillside and through a grove of ragged apple trees that led to a wide lawn. Ahead of them stood a magnificent house made of rough-hewn logs. It was the Walker House, the most popular Bed and Breakfast in the valley and a favorite location for weddings and anniversaries.

"Wow, what a cool house," Charlie said. "It's like a giant log cabin. I wonder who built it."

"Thaddeus Walker," Martin replied. "He was a timber baron in the valley a hundred years ago. He needed a house big enough for his nine children."

The ragged group clomped upon the wide porch to the front door. It was unlocked and Martin walked inside. Andy paused a moment and glanced behind him. He thought he heard something among the apple trees, but saw nothing and assumed his blinky hearing was playing tricks on him.

He dragged his heavy feet into the house behind Charlie and Hector, and closed the heavy door with a reassuring thud.

The lobby was dark, but seemed undamaged. Wagon-wheel chandeliers hung from rough-hewn beams. Rustic bentwood furniture faced an enormous river-rock fireplace.

Martin tried the light switch to no avail. Charlie and Hector flopped into armchairs, exhausted, but Andy followed his dad to the front desk. Martin rang the tiny bell, but no one appeared to greet the new customers.

"Maybe the aliens got them," Andy said.

"Maybe," Martin replied.

"I'll be right back. Don't go anywhere," Charlie said, exiting down a hallway.

"We'll come too," Andy said, eager to explore.

Martin tugged his arm. "No, stay here. She's just going to find a bathroom."

"How do you know?"

"'Cause that's what women mean when they say *I'll be right back*. It's more polite than saying, *I gotta go pee*."

Andy nodded, too tired to explore the issue any further. He rubbed his face and ran his hands through his messy hair. For the first time, his dad noticed the bandages, scrapes, and cuts on his head and arms.

"You're hurt."

"Dad, I'm fine."

Martin dropped to one knee for a better look. Andy braced himself for the all-too-familiar inspection of his face, head, arms and hands. The only consolation was that Charlie wasn't there to witness the humiliating routine.

"Okay, we'll need to get these cuts cleaned and put on some new bandages," Martin said. "Get a fire going. I'll find a first aid kit."

Martin left down the back corridor. Andy wanted to go with him — he'd just found his dad and didn't want to lose him again — but something stopped him. After all his adventures, his dad still treated him as though he were made of breakable china.

He crossed the lobby to the wide fireplace hearth. All the makings for a fire were there — fancy long matches, kindling, a stack of old West Bend Gazette's, and split logs. He opened the fireplace screen, checked the flue, and built a fire for the second night in a row.

Within moments, kindling burned to a steady crackle. Hector kneeled beside him and held out his hands to capture as much heat as possible. Moments later, Charlie returned and they all watched the growing flames. Only the scent of frying bacon pulled them from the fire's warmth. Andy led the way to the kitchen where Martin stood before a large gas stove, cracking eggs into a large bowl. Bacon sizzled in a skillet.

"Bacon," Hector sighed.

"The power is out, but the gas stove still works," Martin said. "Everything in the freezer has thawed, but still passes the smell test."

The kids stood by the stove and watched the bacon cook. It was more than a meal to them, it was hope. If something as familiar as bacon could still exist, then maybe there was a way back to the boring but comfortable lives they once knew. Maybe their families could be found, and West Bend rebuilt, and a new sign installed over the Rialto Theater. Maybe their homes could be repaired and Otter Lane repaved. Maybe Andy could start a new fleet of model spaceships and hang them from the new ceiling of his new bedroom.

"We looked for you," Martin said, stirring the eggs. "The pick-up got through the tunnel... well half of it did. We walked back to find you, but the end was blocked. I knew you must have been thrown clear. I knew that."

"The machine rammed it," Andy said. "They rammed it until a ton of rocks fell down."

"That's what we figured. We had no choice but to go on to Pine Mountain. We walked the rest of the way. The truck was wrecked."

For a moment Andy thought there was something stuck in his dad's eyes given how red and moist they were.

"You were at Pine Mountain?" Charlie asked. "Did you see my mom? Her name is Sharon Ozette."

"There were a lot of people at Pine Mountain," Martin replied. "Soldiers and scientists and refugees fleeing the aliens. I can't say I met your mom, but everyone there is safe. Nothing can get in there. It's cut right into the side of a mountain, you know. Solid rock."

"Is that where all those army trucks came from?" Hector asked. "Is that where they are going back to?"

Martin poured the eggs into another frying pan already sizzling with melted butter. "Yes. The army set up a search party this morning and I volunteered. Then we saw the tripod in town and the cages of people. I'm sure everyone is back at Pine Mountain by now, safe and sound. Now why don't all of you get cleaned up. Andy, first aid kit's on the counter."

Martin nodded to a bright red box beside the large kitchen sink. Andy flipped it open and fished out bandages and antiseptic. Hector and Charlie washed their hands as Andy cleaned and dressed every cut and scrape. The curious glances Charlie gave him did not escape his notice.

Soon, they were all eating bacon, eggs, and toast before the roaring fire in the lobby. Martin explained how the search party had used old logging roads to get around the blocked tunnel and search the neighborhoods around West Bend. They found survivors hiding in basements, wine cellars, and bomb shelters. The convoy even stopped at the blocked tunnel where Martin found the rear axle of his pickup and footprints leading to the Hoffman farm. There he found Andy's note on the kitchen counter.

"You found my note?" asked Andy.

"I sure did," Martin replied, pulling the piece of paper from his pocket. He unfolded it, cleared his throat, and read, "Dear Mr. Hoffman, my name is Andy McBean and I live at 1401 Otter Road. I have eaten three pieces of bread and jam, and drank the rest of your milk. I am borrowing a jacket, shirt, hat, and gloves as there was no time to put mine on when the aliens attacked. I will return them as soon as I find my parents. Best regards, Andy McBean."

Martin folded the note and returned it to his pocket. Andy wondered again if something was caught in his dad's eyes. The fired crackled and sparked. Charlie recounted how Andy had helped her out of her destroyed home. Hector told of being caught by the tripod and separated from his family.

Andy had so much to tell that he didn't know where to begin. Never before had so many interesting things happened to him in such a short span of time. There was the adventure at Charlie's house, the fight with Reggie, fleeing from the alien tripod and falling down the storm drain, and the battle of West Bend. And there was the matter of the dying alien he had saved and how the creature, in turn, had saved him. He didn't know where to begin, knowing any item from the list would draw his dad's face tight with worry.

"I went to your office," he began. "There was a woman there who helped me, but I can't remember her name?"

"What did she look like?" Martin asked.

"She had green eyes."

"That's Linda."

"I didn't get to thank her."

"She's back to Pine Mountain by now," Martin said. "I'm sure she's telling your mom and Freddie about seeing you. We'll hike there tomorrow, taking the river tail around the tunnel. You can thank her then. But it's a long hike and we'll need a good night's sleep."

Andy nodded in approval. Hector yawned and Charlie stretched. They could have had their pick of bedrooms, but no one wanted to leave the warmth of the fireplace. So they brought in pillows and blankets from the linen closet and made beds right on the floor by the hearth. In the flickering light, they settled to sleep, though Martin only rested in a chair, a fire poker within reach for reasons Andy didn't quite understand.

But Andy was perfectly happy not understanding everything. His dad was here and would do all the understanding they needed. As sleep crept upon him, he thought he saw a furry shadow through a window, and three eyes blinking in the firelight.

The evening was cold, but not unpleasant and Been'Tok's fur kept him more than comfortable. The planet's annoying gravity, however, tugged every bone in his body. He crouched on his three legs, settling his weight upon the planks that surrounded the dwelling. The entire structure was made of plant life, perhaps crafted from the tallest trees that grew throughout the valley.

The bipeds were indeed clever.

They were not insignificant life forms as the Masters insisted. True, their spaceships and weapons were crude, but their lack of technical sophistication didn't mean the species was without merit. After all, Been'Tok could assemble and operate a Seeker, but had no idea what made the machines run or how they responded to his every thought.

He wished he could understand the Great Warrior's thoughts. Why had this mightiest of bipeds fixed his jammed respirator and saved his life? As part of the Seeker crew,

Been'Tok had captured many bipeds and damaged many of their dwellings. Why repay such violence with an act that was so... something?

Been'Tok made a note to invent a word to describe what the Warrior had done. He could then use the word to describe his own decision to pull the Warrior away from the falling Seeker. The word could be very useful on this planet.

Been'Tok was tempted to contact the Masters for suggestions, but sensed they would only demand his immediate return to base to resume his menial duties. That was no longer an option. As he lay dying amidst the flowers, he had sworn to never again do menial tasks. Instead, he would endeavor to study the many things that he'd never be taught.

Maybe the Great Warrior could teach him.

CHAPTER TWENTY-TWO

A Fresh Start

That night, Andy dreamed he was back in the hospital. He often dreamed of the hospital, though never about the chemicals that dripped into his veins or the dark days when it looked like they wouldn't work.

He dreamed of the fun times in the children's ward where Paul welcomed him into a small, but tight-knit club of bald-headed kids. They played video games, raced wheel chairs around the nurses' station, and binged on *Three Stooges* and *Marx Brothers* movies.

Paul was the unofficial, but undeniable leader; the referee for their games, the instigator of late-night raids on the vending machines in the waiting room, and the squad commander of their water-fights with the orderlies. And when a storm rumbled outside their hospital room, Paul counted the seconds between the lightning and thunder.

"You scared?" he asked.

"A little," Andy replied.

"You can do this, McBean. A walk in the park. A day at the races. A night at the opera. And when you get better, nothing will stop you."

As the storm raged and thunder fought hand-to-hand with lightning, Andy wasn't so sure.

*

He bolted awake, no longer in the hospital. The lobby of the Bed and Breakfast was lit by just a few glowing embers in the fireplace. Charlie and Hector slept nearby, undisturbed, but the chair his dad had sat in was empty.

Andy saw him through the windows, on the front porch. Martin stared at the distant hills where bolts of lightning flashed. Andy wondered why his dad found the lightning so interesting. Storms were always rumbling through the valley. Andy yawned and settled back into his makeshift bed, reassured his dad was only steps away.

When he woke again, it was to the smell of maple syrup. He rubbed his face and scratched his matted hair. Charlie and Hector were nowhere to be seen. The fire had completely gone out and the lobby was filled with a morning chill.

Andy stood and wrapped himself in a blanket, then slipped into his shoes and followed the sweet scent to the kitchen where his dad was making pancakes at the stove. Charlie and Hector sat at the counter, stuffing their faces.

"Good morning, Andy."

"There he is."

"Hey, sleepy-head."

Andy settled onto a stool beside Hector. The kitchen was large and bright, filled with enough pots and pans to cook for dozens of people. The cheerful scent seemed like a dream. Was it only yesterday that he had been chased by the tripod and survived the battlefield of West Bend? Only the cuts and scrapes on his arms reminded him of his recent adventures, and that he had survived every one of them.

He sat at the counter and smiled for the first time in forever. The worst was behind him. By nightfall he would see his mom and Freddie again. They might already know he was coming. The Army would have returned to Pine Mountain the night before, and those he had freed from the cages would have told them he was alive.

Martin pushed a plate of pancakes and a small pitcher of maple syrup toward him. "Eat up, kiddo. We have a long hike ahead of us."

Andy slathered the pancakes with whipped butter and drowned them in syrup. Hector drew laughs when he folded and stuffed an entire pancake into his mouth. Charlie grew quiet and thoughtful as she stared out the window.

"What are they?" she asked.

"I don't know," Martin replied. "No one knows. Not yet at least. They aren't from this world, that's for certain, and that changes everything. You kids will grow up in a time when we know for sure there is intelligent life beyond our planet."

"What do they want?" Hector mumbled, his mouth full.

"We don't know that either," Martin said. "The officers at Pine Mountain said they've shut down the power networks and communication lines all over the world. I just want you all to know I will do everything I can to keep you safe, but these are dangerous times. We must be careful and look out for each other. Now, what supplies will we need for our hike?"

"I'll need better shoes," Charlie said. "And a heavier coat."

"Check the closets and try to scrounge something up. What else?"

"Food and water," Hector said.

"Good, what else?"

"First aid kit. A knife. Matches for a fire," Andy ticked off. "A compass and a map, and something to carry all this stuff in."

Martin clapped his hands. "Okay then. Let's eat up and get cracking. Daylight's burning."

Half an hour later, a pile of material filled the hearth in the lobby. Charlie had found thick-soled hiking boots in the lost-and-found bin. Andy found a case of bottled water in the pantry, and Hector pulled a variety of coats, hats, and gloves from various closets. Everyone found something that fit and while their appearance was odd and mismatched, they would be warm and dry.

Everything was stuffed into backpacks along with apples, boxes of cookies, and the sandwiches Martin had made.

Finally, they gathered on the back porch and paused as the morning sun glistened off the broad lawn, every blade of grass sparkling with dew.

"Every journey begins with a first step," Martin said.

"Dad, aren't we forgetting something?"

His dad looked puzzled until Andy held up a piece of paper and pencil. Then he smiled and said, "Why don't you write the note, Andy. You're pretty good at it."

Andy addressed the note to owner of the B&B and explained what they had eaten and borrowed, and promised to reimburse them once the alien peril had ended. He left the note on the kitchen counter, beneath a pitcher of maple syrup. Without further delay, Martin lead the way across the damp lawn, Charlie and Hector close behind.

Andy hesitated a moment at the kitchen door, thinking how much he would miss the soft pillows, warm fireplace, and the scent of bacon and pancakes. Something rustled in the garden of azaleas and rhododendrons. He cocked his head for a better listen, but the noise faded and he assumed it was just the wind.

He left the back porch and hurried to catch up to the others. They tramped down a dirt logging road until they reached a wide turn-out just above the Otter River. In the summer, anglers parked here to fish for rainbow trout, but there were no cars today, not on this chilly morning so early in the spring. By the time they stood at the trail head, a light drizzle started to fall. Martin dutifully checked each of his young charges, making sure their coats were zipped and packs snugly fitted.

"Won't do to catch a cold, would it?" he asked, tugged at Andy's jacket.

"Dad, I can do it myself," he said with a glance at Charlie.

Martin smiled. "Off we go then. Andy, you lead the way. I'll bring up the rear. Don't get too far ahead. Everyone stay in sight of one another. Won't do to get lost."

Andy started on the trail through the dense underbrush that lined the river. Tall firs blocked the morning light, but shielded them from the rain. Their boots clomped on the thick loam of leaves and pine needles as the trail followed the river's edge. The burbling current accompanied Charlie's running commentary.

"I've never been in the woods before," she said. "I mean I've been in the woods, but not the real woods. All the trees in Seattle were planted ages ago, so they look like a forest, but they're not a real forest. Not like this. My dad would love this place." She paused the briefest moment, then asked, "Is this the end?"

"No," said Martin. "We've miles to go."

"I don't mean the end of the trail. I mean the end of everything. Civilization as we know it."

"I don't think so. These aliens, wherever they came from, might leave as fast as they arrived."

"Or they might stay forever and make us their slaves," Hector chimed in.

"Is that true?" Charlie asked in a panic. "I don't want to be anyone's slave."

"Hector..."

"I was just kidding."

"We don't know what they want or why they're here," Martin said. "And unless we find a way to communicate with them, we'll never know."

"Andy can talk to them," Charlie offered. "The one that saved you said something."

"Andy, is that true?"

"It spoke, but I couldn't understand it," Andy explained. "My ears were ringing more than usual."

"Your ears ring?" Charlie asked.

"Yeah, ever since I… never mind."

"That tells us they have a language," Martin said. "That's a start."

Andy led the way along the river. He kicking himself for mentioning his hearing. He already sensed that Charlie knew something was wrong with him based on the funny look she had when he bandaged his cuts and scrapes. He knew she would learn about his illness soon enough. Someone at Pine Mountain would tell her. It's not the sort of thing you can keep secret, but Andy hoped it would stay one for as long as possible.

The river foamed white as water sloshed over boulders and fallen trees. Andy recalled the water in the storm drain and how the alien machine had sucked it dry. He knew it was significant, though he wasn't quite sure why. He paused beside boulders worn smooth by centuries of water, suddenly feeling that someone or something was watching him.

He shrugged it off and continued up the trail.

CHAPTER TWENTY-THREE

An Unwelcome Visitor

The trail left the river's edge and began a series of switchbacks through a stand of old timber. This part of the forest had never been logged and the trees were mighty giants, hundreds of years old. Andy wondered if they had witnessed, in their long lives, anything as strange as the alien invasion.

He led the way up the steep hillside, huffing and puffing, his eyes fixed on the narrow trail that wove around trees, over gnarled roots, and through glades of swaying ferns. At the wide corner of one switch back, he finally stopped, exhausted, hands on his knees, and gulped air.

Charlie, neither huffing nor puffing, gave him a wry grin. "I'll take the lead."

Andy was too tired to protest and merely waved a weary hand. Hector walked by, then Martin approached.

"You okay?" he asked.

Andy gasped, "Just… my pack… heavier… than hers."

"We can take a rest if you need it."

"I'm fine."

To prove the point, he jogged up the trail. The truth was he needed a rest, but couldn't stand the idea of Charlie and Hector knowing that.

"Your dad is really protective," Charlie said once he caught up to her.

"Yeah, he uh…"

"My dad doesn't care about stuff like that. He lets me go anywhere I want. I don't even have to tell him where. He totally trusts me."

They walked on as Charlie told him how her dad let her do whatever she wanted, no questions asked, and how her mother was *such a drag* in comparison, making her study and learn about computers. Andy wanted to tell her his own mother was even more protective than his dad, but the most he could squeeze into the conversation was an occasional "Yeah" and "Uh huh."

The trail leveled off at the base of a sheer rock cliff. A final turn brought them to a wide meadow on a sloping ridge. It was a good place to take a breather. Andy and Charlie settled upon a flat boulder in the grassy clearing, and took long gulps from their water bottles. Hector flopped beside them and passed around a box of cookies. Martin arrived and unfolded a map. For a quiet moment, they simply appreciated the view of distant hills, each jagged ridge line painted a lighter shade of blue as they receded to the horizon.

"Pretty," Charlie said.

Andy pointed over the bushes at the edge of the clearing. "You can see Port Cascade from here."

It had been several months since Andy had seen the tall buildings of the distant city, and just the sight of them gave him a shudder. He thought of the hospital and the cancer ward on the fifth floor. There must be a new group of patients there, a new club of bald kids.

The bushes rustled. It was not the wind this time. Something was moving within the thicket of branches.

"You see that?" Andy said, hopping off the rock. "It's him. I'm sure of it."

"Andy, be careful," Martin said.

"He won't hurt us, Dad."

"Andy, come back."

Andy started across the clearing and called, "Come on out. We won't hurt you."

Martin stood upon the rock for a better view. "Andy, come back here, right now."

"I'm fine. Jeez, you never trust me."

Charlie was right; his dad was too protective. Andy was tired of his smothering attention. Hadn't he survived on his own just fine? Hadn't he evaded capture and, even more, freed the hostages from the aliens' cages? Dealing with a shy alien was nothing compared to fleeing from a tripod.

He saw a patch of dark fur within the bushes. Branches rustled again, this time accompanied by a throaty grunt.

Andy crouched low, holding his palms up to show he had no weapon of any kind.

"Come on. It's okay," he said. We won't hurt you."

"Andy, come back," Martin said.

"I think it's working," Andy insisted.

The bushes rustled. Branches cracked and snapped. A large black bear burst into the clearing.

Charlie shrieked.

Hector screamed.

"Andy!" Martin shouted.

The beast roared and swiped its paw across the grass, digging up great clumps of sod. Andy was paralyzed at the sight of the bear's glaring eyes and bared fangs dripping saliva. He struggled to remember what to do when coming face to face with a bear. Don't run. Yell something. Don't run. Stand tall. Don't run. Raise your arms so you appear as big as possible. And whatever you do, don't run.

Andy ran.

Everyone ran. Even Hector dropped the box of perfectly good cookies and bolted across the grassy meadow. They ran away from the bear as fast as their feet would carry them. Only Martin rushed toward Andy, grabbing his arm and pulling him away, following the others toward the base of the cliff.

The bear roared and charged after them. Martin tugged off his backpack and threw it aside, hoping the bear would stop to eat the sandwiches inside. Apparently the beast had a larger meal in mind. It swatted the pack aside with one sweep of a paw.

The clearing ended at a stand of scrawny trees. Charlie and Hector bolted into the grove, Andy and his dad close behind. The branches whipped their faces and tore at their clothes. Charlie and Hector reached a wall of giant boulders piled up at the base of the cliff.

Hector climbed up one boulder. Charlie another. Andy was right behind her and she reached down to pull him up. He lost his footing and slipped, but Martin, in the nick of time, shoved him on top of the boulder.

"Climb higher," he yelled.

"Dad!" Andy shouted, eyes wet with panic.

He had already made the worst mistake a person can make when faced with a bear. He had run when he should have stood his ground. Black bears typically won't attack something that stands its ground, but if something runs, it must be worth chasing… and killing… and eating.

The bear thundered through the trees toward Martin, snapping every branch in its path. There was no time for him to climb the boulders, so he grabbed a rock and threw it. The bear flinched, but kept charging.

"Dad!" Andy yelled again.

He watched helplessly as the bear swatted his dad with a paw the size of a catcher's mitt. The animal bellowed through yellow teeth. Another swipe connected with Martin's ankle. The third sent him falling.

The bear thundered through the trees toward Martin,

snapping every branch in its path.

Andy, terrified, watched the beast stalk toward his dad. "No!" he shouted.

Something dropped from the trees, landing between Martin and the bear. Andy recognized the light brown fur and the dented mechanical harness.

The alien.

The bear, clearing unimpressed with the size of the odd creature, roared and pawed the dirt, declaring to all its power and greatness. Andy thought the alien was done for, but it stood its ground. The flaps on its respirator opened and air whistled through them. The soft folds of its fur filled and expanded.

The creature swelled like an inflatable toy.

When it seemed it could not possibly expand more, it kept growing as more air rushed through its apparatus. Soon, the alien dwarfed the bear and even dwarfed the boulders around it. The bear watched with apprehension, then growled deep and mean. This was his forest and he was not about to be frightened off by a strange animal with three legs and three eyes.

There was a moment of silence, then the alien roared.

All the air it had inhaled was released in a terrifying scream. Its thick lips quavered under the velocity of the air rushing from them. Clouds of dust were stirred up by the resulting wind. Tree branches swayed and snapped. The bear cowered under the deafening blast, its fur flattened and face distorted. Confused and frightened, it turned and ran, fleeing back up the path it had broken through the underbrush and disappearing into the shadows.

Andy climbed down from the boulders and dropped to the dirt beside his dad. Blood darkened the area around Martin's right ankle. His white sock was soaked red and the cuff of his jeans had been shredded. Martin's face was flushed and drawn tight with pain.

"Dad," Andy whispered.

His father didn't look at him, so focused was he on the alien just steps away. Now deflated back to its normal size, the alien looked from Andy to Martin and back again. The mechanism around its shoulders wheezed with each breath. The alien contorted its face into a revolting expression. Martin gasped at the sight.

"It's okay," Andy said. "I think that's what passes for a smile on its planet."

"I'd hate to see what passes for a frown," Martin replied.

CHAPTER TWENTY-FOUR

A New Acquaintance

A ndy knew his father was badly hurt. The scratches inflicted by the bear were so deep that the word scratches hardly seemed sufficient. When the blood and dirt had been washed away with a bottle of water, the wounds only appeared deeper and more serious.

Martin directed Charlie and Hector to search for long branches he could use as crutches, but Andy knew his dad just wanted to spare them the gory sight of his injuries. He stayed by his dad and helped him use antiseptic and bandages from the first aid kit to wrap his ankle.

Through it all, the alien lurked nearby, clearly fascinated by the process. Its three eyes darted from Martin, to the bloody wound, to Andy, then back to Martin again. Martin kept a wary eye on the creature, but there was little else he could do in his present condition.

When his ankle had been tightly wrapped and branches crafted into makeshift crutches, the group made their way back to the grassy clearing. They found the backpack Martin had thrown at the bear, and proceeded onto the trail. Charlie and Hector led the way quietly while Andy stayed close to his dad. The alien ambled not far behind, murmuring croaks and purrs of amazement as it inspected the plants and trees all around.

Charlie nodded toward the creature. "What do we do about… it?"

"Not much we can do," Andy replied.

"We can't just lead it to Pine Mountain."

"It doesn't even have a weapon."

"It might call for help. That big ship could show up again and blast everything. Then what?"

"We have to go to Pine Mountain," Andy said firmly. "My dad needs a doctor."

By mid-day the trail took them back along the banks of the Otter River where they rested on fallen trees bleached white by the sun. Martin proclaimed it a fine place for lunch and raised his leg upon a log. Charlie passed out sandwiches and apples, each a bit banged up from their journey. Hector devoured his lunch all the same. Andy took a bite of his sandwich and watched the alien stare at the rushing water. In a burst of confidence, he approached the creature, holding out his apple.

"Andy, what are you doing?" Charlie asked.

"Seeing if he's hungry."

"You don't even know what he eats," Hector mumbled.

"You don't even know if he's a he," Charlie added. "It could be a girl alien. Well, it could."

Undeterred, Andy approached the creature. Its larger eye opened so wide that Andy could see his own reflection in the dark iris. The giant eyeball studied the apple. Andy bit into his sandwich to demonstrate eating and the meaning was apparently made clear. The alien reached out a three-fingered hand and took the apple.

He, she, or it studied the fruit a moment, then popped the entire thing in its wide mouth. Everyone watched as it chewed the apple and made a satisfied purr.

"I think he likes it," Hector said.

The alien stopped chewing and said something that sounded like, "Bat nak no tan."

Andy gasped. Hector and Charlie froze, mouths open. Even Martin sat up, wincing at the pain.

"It spoke," Andy said. "Did you hear that? It spoke!"

"Maybe it's hungry. Maybe it wants more apples."

"Ask it why they're here. What do they want?"

"Okay, okay, everybody be quiet," Andy said. He pointed to himself and said, "Andy."

The alien said nothing. Andy pointed to his dad, Charlie, and Hector and said their names. The creature watched him curiously, then lumbered toward Andy. It pointed to him and said in a gravelly voice, "Adee."

Charlie shouted with glee. Hector jumped up and down. Martin propped himself on his elbows for a better view.

"That's right, Andy," Andy said.

"Addy," the alien repeated.

"Andy."

"Atty."

"Andy."

"Anby."

"Andy."

"Amby."

"Say it really slow," Charlie advised.

Andy looked right at the alien and said slowly, "An-dy"

The alien leaned toward him and repeated, "An-Dee."

Andy whooped. Hector and Charlie high-fived each other. Martin clapped. Andy *shhh'd* them again and pointed to the alien. Everyone stared at the creature with anticipation. The alien raised its head, spread one hand upon his chest and said, "Been'Tok."

"Bentack," Andy repeated.

"Been'Tok."

"Been'take."

"Been'Tok."

"Ben'tack?"

"Been'Tok"

"Been'tick."

The alien raised both large hands to Andy, leaned forward, and said slowly, "Beeeen-Tok."

Andy listened carefully and replied in his best impersonation of the alien's clipped language, "Been'Tok."

The creature purred and contorted its face into the familiar grotesque expression. Everyone gasped.

"There's that face again," Martin said.

"We're going to have to work on that," Andy noted.

With a glance at his watch, Martin stood on his good foot and positioned his crutches under his arm. "Let's keep going. We want to make the base by nightfall."

They stood and gathered their things, picked up their garbage, and slung their packs over their shoulders. Charlie led the way up the trail, followed by Hector, Andy, the alien, and Martin, who brought up the rear, his bandaged foot swaying with each step. Andy stayed close to his dad, concerned at the pale look on his face and the sweat beading on his forehead.

The alien pointed to everything they passed and croaked its alien name.

"Nan'tok."

"Tree," Andy said.

"Nan mak."

"Dirt."

"To'Dash."

"Rock."

A gentle rain began to fall.

"Rain," Andy said, pointing to the sky.

He waited for Been'Tok to respond, but the alien merely looked upward, marveling at the falling drops.

"Maybe they don't have a word for rain," Hector suggested.

"Maybe they don't have rain," Charlie added.

Andy pulled his hat tight to his head. Charlie and Hector tugged their hoods snug. Martin flipped the wings of his hat around his ears. Andy tried to imagine a planet without rain. All his life he had known rain. Hardly a day went by, it seemed, when something wasn't dripping on his head. As much as he hated rain, he knew a planet without it must be a very sad place to live.

Been'Tok learned that in the biped language, *Great Warrior* is pronounced *An'Dee*. Its companions are called *Hec'Tor* and *Char'Lee* and the largest biped, clearly the Warrior's servant and guardian, is called *Mar'Tin*.

Mar'Tin had been grievously injured by the wild beast. Red liquid seeped from its wounds and it could only hobble with the aid of long sticks. How the bipeds coped with only two legs was a mystery.

The Masters would never tolerate such an injury. A hobbled Worker would be abandoned or vaporized by the nearest Guardian, its water collected for the common good.

But An'Dee was clearly concerned with his servant's well-being. There was something about the relationship that captivated Been'Tok even more than the plants and trees around him. Clearly, another new word was needed.

CHAPTER TWENTY-FIVE

Hopes Dashed

The group walked through the forest, listening to the gentle patter of rain upon the leaves of wild berry bushes. The trail opened onto a great slide of rocks and boulders, now slick with rain. Charlie picked the safest way through the bramble and into another dense grove of trees.

"Hold up," Martin called out. He pointed one crutch at the rocky cliff where the stone had been worn smooth by eons of falling water.

Andy stopped. "What is it?"

"The falls. There should be falls here. This time of year the water should be rushing over that cliff."

They pressed on through the trees and the gentle shower ended, replaced by brilliant shafts of sunlight that set the misty air aglow. The grove thinned and Charlie stopped at the edge of a large meadow. Everyone gathered around her as a break in the clouds let sunlight wash over a broad field of wildflowers. Dapples of red and yellow mixed with purple and orange. Been'Tok gasped, eyes wide and hands flexing with excitement. The alien lumbered into the field, ambling from one colorful patch to the next.

"He really likes flowers," Andy explained.

The alien returned with a bouquet and said, "An'Dee."

Charlie smirked, "I think he likes you."

Andy took the flowers and held them under his nose. He breathed deeply, taking in their scent. "You have to smell them," he said, handing the flowers back.

"How's it gonna do that without a nose?" Hector asked.

He was right. Where Been'Tok's nose should be was just a patch of fur. Andy noticed the vents on the respirator and moved the flowers to them. They opened and closed, but no reaction was evident on the creature's face.

"I don't think he can smell them, son," Martin said. "I think that device filters the air."

Andy held the flowers back under his own nose and pantomimed the act of breathing, then handed them back to Been'Tok. The alien twisted a latch on the side of the mechanical shawl. The device clicked open and fell to his feet. The creature looked oddly naked without it. Its fur was matted where the device had rested and where the vents had been, slender gills opened and closed.

Been'Tok held the bouquet beside his gills and the flaps of skin opened as air rushed in, drawing the flowers toward them. The alien purred. Its eyes grew wide and it staggered at the bliss of the scent.

He breathed deep again and again, drunk on the perfume. Hector laughed and Charlie clapped, but Andy's smile faded as Been'Tok's swaying became a stagger. The alien stumbled. Charlie and Hector only laughed harder, believing the antics were playful clowning, but Andy knew it was no act. He'd seen the look in the creature's heavy eyes before.

"Something's wrong," he said.

Been'Tok fell onto the meadow. Andy rushed forward. He kneeled beside the alien just as he had in the flower shop, and saw the same desperation in the creature's fluttering eyes. Its lips drained of color and body flattened as though deflating. Martin joined Andy at the creature's side.

"What wrong with him, dad?"

"Something's made him sick."

"The flowers?"

"I don't know. We need to get him back in his harness."

Andy grabbed the device lying nearby. It was far heavier that it appeared and Hector came to his aid, but Charlie stood her ground.

"Help us!" Andy yelled.

She finally helped them drag the harness to Been'Tok. They lifted the alien into it and fastened it closed over his shoulders. The machine tightened around the alien and its vents clicked open and closed.

They waited and watched.

And watched and waited.

With a gasp, Been'Tok breathed again. Its eyes fluttered

open and the color returned to its lips. It stood, swaying a moment, then finding balance. Andy noted that three legs were very handy in such situations.

"That was scary," Hector said. "I thought he was a goner. It was like he was fine one minute then all bonky the next."

"I think there's something in our air that makes him sick," Martin said. "Maybe a virus or microbe."

"Why doesn't it make us sick?" Charlie asked.

"We're used to it," Martin replied. "Our bodies have developed immunity."

Andy glared at Charlie. "Why didn't you help us? He could have died."

"It's not a pet," she shot back. "It's the enemy!"

She stomped across the colorful meadow. Hector shrugged and started after her, but Andy stayed close to Martin and Been'Tok, unsure who might need his help more. The alien lumbered on slowly and Martin had only grown paler, the strain of each step evident on his face.

The sound of a yelp, and then laughter, drew their attention. Catching up to Hector, they found him standing at the rim of a deep pit. He snickering at Charlie, who had fallen into it. The wildflowers around her were flattened as though pressed in a scrapbook.

"Get me outta here," Charlie said, reaching up to them.

Andy just folded his arms, happy to give her a dose of her own medicine. Hector took her hand and helped her out. As she brushed the dirt off her pants and jacket, Andy noted the shape of the depression. There was something familiar about it. He jogged off to the left and was soon lost in the tall meadow.

"Andy, don't go far," Martin called out.

He didn't have to go far. Just a few paces away, Andy found another depression perfectly cut into the soft soil.

"Here's another one!" he called.

The others joined him at the rim of the depression.

"It's them, isn't it?" Charlie asked.

"I think so," Martin nodded.

They followed the tripod footprints, one to the next, and soon arrived at the rocky shore of Duck Lake. At least it had been Duck Lake. Now it was just a wide muddy pit, drained of all water. They stared at the great expanse of cracked mud, flecked here and there with the silver bodies of dead fish.

Andy watched Been'Tok shake mud off its feet. "I think I know what they want," he said. "It's the water. They want our water."

"How do you figure that?" Martin asked.

"When the tripod chased us, I hid in a storm drain. It chased me into a big catch basin and later sucked up all the water. Every drop of it."

"Just like the falls."

"And this lake," Charlie added.

Hector looked up to the rain clouds. "If they want water. They've come to the right place."

"Maybe they ran out of water on the planet they came

from," Andy speculated. "And now they have to go from planet to planet to find more."

"They can't do that, can they?" Hector asked. "Take all our water? What would we drink?"

"If they were here..." Martin said, his voice trailing off.

He hurried along the shore of the lake, leading the way up the trail with renewed energy, hobbling as fast as his branch-crutches allowed.

"Hey, where's he going?" Charlie asked.

The others struggled to keep up. Martin didn't stop until the trail ended at the Old Mill Road. They all stood on the pavement and caught their breath. Even Charlie huffed and puffed, her face flushed. Been'Tok seemed particularly fascinated with the entrance to the tunnel down the hill, and the front half of the McBean pickup resting nearby.

Martin hobbled in the opposite direction. There was something about the determination of his stride and the tense posture of his shoulders that told Andy something was terribly wrong. Around a sharp bend in the road, their faces fell at the sight far ahead. The valley ended in a vast horseshoe, the road widening where it met the cliff-side entrance to the Pine Mountain Army Base. Where trucks and artillery had once rested, however, there was only a dark tangle of smoldering ruins.

Andy's hopes faded in an instant. There would be no tearful reunion with his mom and Freddie. No warm bed or hot food. No chance to thank the woman with green eyes.

The army he hoped would drive away the aliens lay in ruin. There would be no rebuilding, and things would never be as they had been.

Was everyone dead? It was too horrible to contemplate. Martin stepped forward, but his feet failed him and he stumbled. He staggered on, the others close behind, eyes glued to the smoking battlefield up the road. The scene took on more grim detail with every step. The molten wreckage of artillery and trucks stained the road pitted with footprints of several tripods.

One alien machine, its silver body dented from repeated blasts, had fallen right across the parking lot. Another leaned against the stone cliff as though merely catching its breath, one leg severed at the hip. The base's giant blast doors, cut right into the mountainside and big enough to drive trucks through, had been punctured and twisted open like a sardine can. There was no motion, no sign of life, just rising tendrils of black smoke.

"Mom," Charlie whispered. "Mom!"

"Stay back," Martin said.

"Dad…"

"I said stay back," Martin repeated firmly.

Andy watched his dad limp into the wreckage. The sun paused above the western ridge, sending long shadows across the landscape. Charlie started to cry. Been'Tok was fascinated by her tears, but she shoved the alien away.

Andy scratched his head and rubbed his face. He started

forward, Charlie, Hector, and Been'Tok right behind him. They walked through plumes of acrid smoke, making their way around the charred wreckage of vehicles and weapons. Some army trucks had been crushed under tripod feet, others melted into truck-shaped puddles of hardened metal. Andy knew his father didn't want them to see the grisly sights of battle, but there were no bodies in the wreckage. The base was empty.

CHAPTER TWENTY-SIX

Pine Mountain

ndy, Hector, and Charlie picked their way through the battlefield. The smoke cleared around them, revealing Martin sitting on a pile of rocks in the shadow of the leaning tripod.

"There's your dad," Hector said, pointing.

"Stay here," Andy replied.

Andy approached Martin, who faced away from him, his head low and shoulders slumped. "Dad?"

"I told you to wait."

His father's voice cracked and Andy knew what he had feared was true — his dad was crying. He had never seen his dad cry before. Never even thought such a thing was possible. His dad built buildings and houses. His dad drove a pickup. Yet his shoulders heaved and he made sniffling noises. This was worse than a thousand wrecked army trucks and cannons.

Andy kept his distance. He didn't like anyone to see him

cry, and would do anything to find privacy in his room or the forest when his emotions bubbled up. Something drew him to his father, however, and he wrapped an arm around the man's shoulders. They were as wide as he remembered, but somehow drained of strength.

"The aliens must have followed the army trucks back here," Martin said.

"Mom? Freddie?"

"The place is empty. The aliens must have taken everyone. Picked them up with those tentacles."

"Where did they take them?"

"I don't know."

"We have to find them," Andy said. "Freddie will be scared. Mom will be worried."

Martin leaned against Andy. His weight became heavier until Andy couldn't support him any longer and Martin slumped upon the rocks, unconscious.

"Dad!" Andy yelled.

Charlie and Hector ran forward, stunned at the sight of Martin's ashen face and limp form. Been'Tok lagged behind, more interested in the tripod leaning against the cliff.

"What happened?" Charlie asked. She tugged at Martin's jacket. "Wake up! Wake up!"

"He passed out," Andy replied.

Charlie tugged at Martin's shirt. She shook his shoulders, desperate, but there was no response. Martin lay breathing but motionless.

Andy didn't know what to do when someone passes out and the one person who could tell him had passed out. Tears welled in his eyes. He clenched his fist. Sometimes the bite of his fingernails into his palm chased the tears away. He could not cry now. There was no pillow to bury his face into, and running into the wild was not an option.

Something squealed near the blast door and everyone froze at the sound. Even Been'Tok trained his smaller eyes on the giant metal doors. The holes punched into them were high off the pavement, but the squeal was low to the ground and sounded like the feedback on the school's public address system. Andy ran toward the sound and found the source in a small communications panel to one side of the blast doors. There were buttons, a speaker, a camera lens, and a keypad with numbers and letters. Andy pushed them all.

"Hello!" he shouted. "Is anyone there? We need help!"

Silence.

"Hello!" Andy yelled again. "My father is hurt. He needs help. Open the door."

The speaker crackled and squealed. "Go away," a thin voice replied.

"Someone's in there," Hector shouted. He joined Andy at the intercom and shouted right into the dark lens of the camera, "Open up! We need help!"

"It isn't safe," the voice replied. "I can't let you in. Not with those things still out there. Go away!"

Andy glanced at Been'Tok who stood beneath the

Andy ran toward the sound and found the source in a small
communications panel to one side of the blast doors.

damaged tripod. "It won't hurt you. It helped us. It saved our lives."

"I'm sorry," the voice replied. "I can't let you in. Now go away!"

The speaker fell silent.

"Hello?" Andy yelled. "Hello?"

He stepped to the nearby metal doors and pounded his fists against them. His small hands created mute thuds that echoed from the torn openings high overhead. If only he could reach the holes, he could crawl inside and find the man with the raspy voice and demand his help. But the openings were too high.

"Do you have a ladder?" Hector asked, also looking at the holes.

"Yes, I packed one in my back pack," Andy shot back. "Of course I don't have a ladder! Why do you ask such stupid questions?"

Hector, chastened, walked back to Charlie and Martin. Andy slumped to his knees and placed his hands flat on the cold pavement. He struggled to organize his thoughts. The sun was setting. They would need shelter and a fire. His dad must be kept warm and his wounds needed fresh bandages.

He felt tears of desperation well up, but clenched his fists again. He must be strong. He remembered how his father had always been there for him during the months of treatment in the hospital. When the news was good, he would bring ice cream or a new model kit to celebrate. When the news was bad, he would rub Andy's shoulders to cheer him up. Andy could almost feel his father's encouraging hands, but when reached for them, he only felt cold metal.

A tentacle grabbed him!

Andy yelped and crawled away. The tentacle extended up to the tripod that leaned against the cliff. Where it attached to the belly of the machine, was a glass bubble. Inside the turret sat Been'Tok. The alien waved.

Andy sighed in relief and let the tentacle pick him up and carry him away from the giant doors. The silver appendage seemed to have a mind of its own, and set him down gently at his father's side. It tousled his hair, then faced the blast doors. With remarkable speed, it shot at the door, punching a hole right where Andy had stood. Metal groaned as the tentacle pulled the opening wide.

"C'mon!" Andy said. "We can get inside."

They lifted Martin's arms and grabbed his legs. By the time they carried him to the opening, Been'Tok had climbed down from the Tripod and joined the effort. They carried Martin into the darkness. Andy couldn't see much of anything, but the echoes of their steps told him the space was large. Dim lights flickered overhead and he made out stone walls and concrete beams. Piled here and there were scattered blankets, discarded pillows, and overturned cots. He wondered which one his mom and Freddie has slept on.

"This is the armory," Charlie said, her voice echoing off the stone walls. "They keep the vehicles and weapons here."

"What's with all the beds and stuff?" Hector asked.

"They must have moved the trucks and cannons out and used this place for all the survivors," Andy replied.

Straight ahead, a set of doors was cut into one wall, lights glowing in their small inset windows. They set Martin upon the cold floor before them. Andy tried the doors and found them locked.

"Open up!" he yelled, pounding on the doors.

Silence.

"Open the doors or we'll break them open!"

Scuffling footsteps approached, accompanied by a jangling sound. Andy backed away as a dark figure filled one window. The door rattled and clicked open, revealing a man dressed in tattered coveralls like those worn by an auto mechanic. A giant ring of keys dangled at his hip. His face was gaunt and dirty, but his hair neatly combed. He squinted at them as though seeing people for the first time.

"Who…. Who are you?" the man asked.

"My name is Andy McBean. My father was hurt by a bear. Will you help us?"

"I… no…. There's no one…. I can't."

Charlie stepped forward, angry. "My name is Charlie Ozette. My mom works here. Let us in!"

"Not with that… That thing!"

Andy grabbed the door before the man could shut it. They struggled, Andy and Hector pushing the door open and the man pushing it closed. Andy wedged a foot into the narrow opening. There was no way he would let the door close again.

"It's okay," Hector yelled. "It's our… prisoner! Yeah, it's our prisoner. We captured it!"

"Captured? Prisoner?" the man stammered.

"Yes, and we've brought it here to learn its secrets."

"Yes… secrets. They have secrets."

"Will you help us?" Andy asked.

"Yes. Yes, I can do that."

The man let go of the door. Andy pushed it open and they carried Martin through. The skinny man made no move to help them, but led the way down a wide corridor. Its painted walls, fluorescent lights, and linoleum floor were familiar and comforting after the long hike through the forest.

"They have lights. Power," Hector noted.

"Must be generators," Charlie said. "My mom said this place has everything."

"What's your name?" Andy asked the man.

"My name? My name? They call me Keys," he replied, jangling the ring on his belt. "I can open any door. Bertha or Lucy or Sally. I name all the doors and the keys that open them, or lock them. Helps me remember."

"Keys, is there a doctor here?"

"No, there's no one. They were all taken." He pointed at Been'Tok. "Taken by them!"

Keys led them to a door marked *Infirmary*. Inside were metal tables and counters, and glass cabinets filled with medical supplies. They set Martin on a table and Keys used scissors to cut away his shredded pant leg and remove his shoe and sock. Blood dribbled from the hiking boot onto the floor. Hector and Charlie stepped back, but Andy stayed right beside his dad.

"They came last night," Keys said as he cleaned the wound with gauze and antiseptic. "The convoy had just returned. Everyone ran outside to greet them. People hugging and kissing. Families reunited. Everyone was so happy."

His voice drifted off again as he stared into space.

"What happened to everyone, Keys?" Charlie asked.

His eyes flicked on again. His expression changed as though a switch had been flipped. "Those lights beyond the clouds. And tentacles reaching down, setting down tripods that snatched up people and put them in cages. The general tried to fight back. Opened up with those big cannons. Did you see? Did you see the ones we got?"

"There was thunder and lightning last night," Andy said, remembering the storm that had awakened him.

"Not thunder. Those were our cannons. And not lightning. That was the tripods and their green death rays."

"But you destroyed them," Hector said. "We saw the machines outside."

"We got two of them. Took one out at the knees and over it goes. That's their weak spot, their legs. But there were more." His voice drifted off again and his eyes darted about as though he was no longer standing over Martin, but reliving the past horror. After a moment, his vision snapped back to the here-and-now and he resumed his work, wrapping fresh bandages around Martin's ankle.

"Madness," he whispered. "The laughter and cheers turned to screams and crying as everyone tried to hide, running around like ants. That's what we are to them. A bunch of ants that they scoop up with their tentacles. The battle was over in minutes. The rest was just screaming as tentacles carried everyone up into the sky."

"Everyone but you," Charlie noted.

"I hid in a supply closet," Keys replied. "I can open any door in the base. Naomi, or Clara, or Margaret. And I can lock them too. I hid. I'm not ashamed to say it. I survived. That's the only thing we can do now. Survive. You'll see."

CHAPTER TWENTY-SEVEN

The Infirmary

Keys wanted to lock Been'Tok in a prison cell, but Andy insisted the alien remain at his side for *interrogation*. Grumbling and muttering, the strange man took Charlie and Hector to rooms where they could clean up. Later, Charlie returned with a bowl of hot soup for Andy and an apple for the alien.

Andy spent the night in the infirmary beside his dad. Even with most of the lights turned off, he couldn't sleep. When Martin's breathing grew weak, Andy scrambled to his side and held his hand. It felt strange to be awake and well while his dad was hurt and unconscious. It was only a year ago that their positions were reversed and Martin was at Andy's side through his treatment.

Andy remembered little of those darkest days when he drifted in and out of consciousness. There was the chorus of chirping machines, the sound of alarms beeping, and nurses and doctors shouting. He felt their hands on him in the darkness, but mostly he remembered Paul at his bedside saying, "You can do this, McBean. Piece of cake. And when you get better, you really will be better."

Andy didn't understand what Paul meant. Of course Andy would be better when he got better. That's what getting better meant. But it wasn't easy and there were moments when Andy couldn't even remember any of the things that would make getting better worthwhile. All he felt was a drifting ache and a desire for the whole thing to be over with.

Been'Tok ambled across the infirmary to Andy's side. The alien glanced from Andy to Martin and back again, trying to puzzle out the relationship.

"Father," Andy said, pointing to Martin. He tapped himself and said, "Son."

"An'Dee," Been'Tok croaked.

"Yes, that's right. But I'm his son. He's my father."

The alien blinked, confused. Andy stepped to a nearby chair over which his jacket was draped, and searched the pockets for his mom's phone. He turned on the device and swiped the screen until he found snapshots of the McBean family. One showed himself as an infant in his dad's arms. He held the screen up so Been'Tok could study the image with all three eyes.

"See? Father," Andy said. "Dad."

Andy swiped the screen to find another photo of himself and Martin fishing, and another of the entire McBean family taken by a fancy photographer in Port Cascade. Been'Tok purred, then pressed a flat finger against his metal shawl. A cloud of sparks swirled before him. Andy gasped as the sparks coalesced into a hologram of Been'Tok standing on an alien world, surrounded by pink trees and purple bushes.

Andy walked around the three-dimensional image, marveling at the detail. Been'Tok waved his hand again and the image scattered, then reassembled into a picture of the alien sitting at a control station surrounded by tentacles.

Again and again the alien waved his hand, shuffling from one image to another, finally stopping at one depicting himself, much younger, in the arms of a machine. Around him similar machines held other alien infants, their furry faces looking up at their mechanical nannies.

"Fa'ther," Been'Tok said.

Andy pondered the strange idea of being raised by a machine. It would have some benefits. A machine would not overreact and go over the deep end. A machine would study the facts and make decisions based on logic and not emotion. A machine might even realize he was better and ready to play soccer again. But would a machine care? Would a machine run through a burning town looking for him, or sit by his hospital bed when he was sick?

Andy smiled and said, "Yes… father."

Been'Tok tried to smile, but it came off as a grimace.

"Smile," Andy said, pointing to his mouth.

The alien tugged his face in various directions, but none came close to resembling a smile.

Andy put the cell phone away. "Let me help."

He pulled at the alien's mouth and tugging its cheeks apart, but nothing worked. The alien's expression looked as though he'd eaten something sour.

"Keep working on that," Andy said.

His head throbbed. He staggered to the bathroom and dampened a washcloth in the sink. Someone appeared right behind him.

"What!?" he gasped, then laughed.

It wasn't another person, merely his own reflection in the mirror on the door, but it may as well have been a stranger. Andy hardly recognized himself. His clothes were torn and ragged. There were more scrapes, cuts, bangs, and bruises on his face and arms than he could count. Even his wild hair seemed battered and bent. If hair could feel pain, his would be screaming.

But he didn't just look different. He was different. The look in his eyes was different. The boy in the family photos was no longer present in his reflection. And much like his bedroom, he knew that no amount of effort would restore him to how he had been just days before.

*

Silence woke him.

With a gasp, Andy sat up on his gurney and looked to his dad, relieved at the rise and fall of Martin's breathing.

There were no windows and no daylight to mark the dawn, but the clock on the wall read half past seven. Been'Tok was nowhere to be seen.

He decided to get something to eat. Down the corridor, the mess hall was filled with empty tables set in neat rows before an equally empty buffet counter. Hector and Charlie, sitting at one table, jumped as he came through the door.

"Oh, it's just you," Hector said.

"We thought it was… him," Charlie added.

"Who?" Andy asked.

"Keys."

"Oh."

"Didn't you hear him last night? He was jangling up and down the hall outside our rooms." Hector said. "That guy is weird. He's not right in the head."

"He's traumatized," Charlie said.

"What?"

"Traumatized. It happens to some people who go through a really bad experience, like a battle."

"How do you know?" Andy asked.

"Uh, my mom told me about it," she replied, then quickly asked, "How's your dad?"

"The same. Still sleeping. What'ya got there?"

Andy pointed to a framed photo sitting on the table beside Charlie. She held up the picture of herself and a woman with matching hair and eyes. Charlie wrapped her arms around the picture.

"It's my mom," she said. "I found it in her office. So creepy. It's like everyone just got up from their desks to greet the survivors. They left behind coffee cups and half eaten sandwiches like they expected to come back any minute."

"I'm sure your mom is okay," Andy said. "And your dad."

"You don't know that."

"I feel it. Just like I feel my mom and brother are okay. And that my dad will get better."

"But you don't know."

"No, I guess I don't."

"I just want it over," she mumbled. "I just want things back the way they were."

"I don't think that's gonna happen," Andy said. "I don't think that's possible. The way things were is like a planet on the other side of the galaxy. We can't get there from here."

"Andy, you hungry?" Hector asked.

"Starved. What's for breakfast?"

"Whatever you want," Hector smiled. "Check this out."

He pulled Andy from the table, leaving Charlie behind, and led him around the buffet counter and through the doors beyond. Bright fluorescent lights lit up the largest kitchen Andy had ever seen. It was even larger than the kitchen at the Bed and Breakfast. Stainless steel ovens, stoves, and refrigerators lined the walls. Pots and pans hung from racks, and dishes and utensils were neatly arranged on shelves.

"This place has everything," Hector said.

He flung open a refrigerator door revealing packs of eggs,

bricks of cheese, and gallons of milk. A freezer was filled with lunch meats, steaks, and chicken patties. Other coolers and freezers were equally stuffed, pantries brimmed with canned goods, and cupboards were stacked with boxes of cereal and bags of flour, sugar, and salt.

"Keys is right, there's enough food here to last for years," Andy marveled.

He made himself a fried ham sandwich on toast slathered with mayonnaise. It looked so good that Hector made one for himself. When they had finished their meal at the commissary table, their stomachs fuller than they'd been in days, Hector belched. Andy wasn't far behind and burped so loud they all broke up laughing. It was the first time Andy had laughed in days, but a wave of guilt swept over him at the thought of his dad in the infirmary, and his mom and Freddie carried off to points unknown.

The doors across the commissary burst opened. Everyone jumped. Keys poked his head inside, scowled at the sound of laughter, then let the doors swing shut. Andy looked to Charlie, who looked to Hector, who shrugged again.

"He was moving stuff all night," Charlie said.

"What's he up to?" Hector asked.

Andy pushed his plate away. "Let's find out."

He crossed the large mess hall and pushed the doors open. On the floor of the corridor, electrical wires ran to the doors at the far end. The trio followed the wires back into the armory. Fresh air and light from the openings in the blast doors filled the chamber. The battle damage was worse than Andy had thought, with walls scraped by tentacles and pocked by gunfire. The severed end of a one tentacle lay on the cement. Cots, pillows, and blankets had been piled into a makeshift barricade.

The electrical wires ended at the blast doors where Keys worked beside a stack of boxes. Andy didn't recognize the words stenciled on the sides of the crates, but knew the symbols for *flammable* and *danger*.

"Good morning, Keys," Andy said.

Keys barely glancing at them. "Morning."

He used a knife to cut away the wire's plastic insulation, then wrapped the exposed copper inside around two metal terminals on one container. Andy looked out the jagged hole in the blast door. It was raining and misty. Been'Tok stood under the leaning tripod. The alien waved its strange hands, directing two tentacles that dragged a tripod leg from one damaged machine to the other.

"Good morning, Been'Tok," Andy waved.

"An'Dee," the alien replied.

"So you're on a first name basis with that thing?" Keys grumbled. "Thought you said it was your prisoner? Shouldn't it be in chains or something?"

"He's... uh... not that kind of prisoner," Hector said.

Keys shrugged. "Doesn't matter. Let him do his thing. I'll do mine. This is the one door I can't lock anymore. Big Bertha. They pealed her open like a sardine can. But not for long."

Keys crossed back across the armory, Andy and the others followed, curious. They passed through the inner doors and walked down the corridor, past the infirmary and the commissary, following the wires on the floor. Around a corner and down a side hall, the wires ended beside a small electrical device.

"What's that?" Hector asked.

"That's the trigger," Keys replied with no more concern than if he'd said *shoes* or *spaghetti sauce.*

"Trigger for what?" Charlie asked, her voice and eyebrows rising with concern.

"For the explosives," Keys replied. "How else can I blow up the entrance?

CHAPTER TWENTY-EIGHT

A Crazy Idea

"Blow it up?" Andy asked. "If you blow it up, how will we get out?"

Keys kneeled by the trigger device and stripped the plastic insulation from the wires, revealing the copper core. "Getting out isn't the issue. Stopping them from getting in is the issue."

Andy traded looks with Charlie and Hector. Was Keys serious? Did he really intend to blow up the entrance and seal them all inside? Andy wanted to say something, but wasn't quite sure what words to use. For days he had wanted to find an adult, any adult, to take charge, make decisions, and do all the things that needed to be done. With his dad unconscious, that responsibility fell to Keys, but Andy now had serious doubts about the man's qualifications.

"Let me get this straight," Charlie started. "You're going to blow up the big doors?"

"No, of course not," Keys replied.

"Oh, good."

"I don't have enough explosives to destroy Bertha," the man went on. "So I'm going to blow up the cliff around her."

"But that's crazy!" Charlie shouted. "That could bring the whole mountain down on our heads."

"Oh, are you an expert in explosives?" Keys asked.

"No, are you?" she shot back.

Keys waved the question aside. "That's beside the point. I've seen this sort of thing done plenty of times. I know just what to do. This wire goes into that thing and the other end goes into that box do-hickey and then we get way back and yell *all clear* and *fire in the hole* and push that button. It's all very simple."

Hector scratched his head. "But how will we get out?"

"Get out? Why would we want to get out? We have everything we need here. We can stay here for years, maybe decades. This place was designed for that. There's food and water and pumps to circulate the air and generators for power. If we play our cards right, we could survive in here for the rest of our lives, maybe longer."

"My mom is out there," Andy said. "And my brother."

"And my mother."

"And my family."

"I'm sorry!" Keys shouted. "But this isn't about moms and brothers and families. This is about our species! This is about the human race! And Big Bertha is the only door I can't lock!"

Andy rubbed his face vigorously and scratched his head to jog some idea loose. It didn't work. Hector and Charlie looked at him expectantly. It was the first time anyone had looked to him for guidance. Usually he was the one waiting for someone to tell him what to do.

He wished his dad were awake. He wanted to run to the infirmary and revive him, but it would be too late by then. Keys would press the trigger and half the mountain would collapse into the armory. And then they would be trapped. Trapped forever. This was wrong and he knew it. He felt it in his gut.

"No!" he shouted and dove at Keys.

He tackled the man around the waist, toppling him to the floor. Charlie joined the scrum, diving on them both. Hector backed away, unsure what to do. Finally, Charlie scrambled to her feet, grabbed the wire from the trigger device, and ran down the corridor, taking it with her. Keys stood and grabbed Andy with one hand and Hector with the other.

"You kids don't understand," he said, pulling them down the hall. "I've been thinking about this a lot and it's all clear to me. The old world is over. And it's never coming back. We have to accept that, cause if we don't, if we try and get things back to where they were, we'll lose. We have to accept that life isn't about living anymore, it's about surviving. And when the aliens come back and can't get in, you'll thank me. You'll say, *Keys, we were wrong and you were right. Thank you for saving our lives.* That's what you'll say."

He opened a door marked 'Maintenance,' and pushed Andy and Hector inside. The small room was filled with mops and brooms and shelves of cleaning supplies. Andy tumbled into a floor polisher and Hector landed on a stack of brooms.

Keys stood in the doorway, silhouetted by the dim light in the corridor. "You'll see. This is the only way."

He slammed the door shut, plunging the closet into darkness. A key rattled in the lock. Andy ran to the door, feeling its cold metal more than seeing it, and slammed his fist against it, but the jangling receded down the hallway.

"Let us out!" he yelled.

Hector joined him at the door and together their fists created a cacophony of banging. They yelled until they were hoarse, but heard nothing but their own shouts.

Andy glared at Hector. "Why didn't you help us?"

"I was gonna. I was gonna give him my banshee yell."

"Your banshee yell? This famous banshee yell that I've *never* heard? That banshee yell? God, you're so stupid."

"I'm not stupid."

"You asked me if I had a ladder."

"Okay, that was stupid. Sometimes I don't know what I'm saying until I've already said it."

The jangling approached again. The keys rattled in the lock and door flew open. Keys stood over them, this time holding Charlie by one arm.

"Stop it, you jerk!" she shouted.

Keys pushed her in and she landed face-first on the dirty end of a mop. "Here's your friend. You'll be safe here. This is where I hid when they came. I could hear everyone outside, screaming and shouting. They begged me to unlock the doors and let them in, but I knew that would be the end of everything. And I was right, because I'm here and they're not. You'll see. When I blow the entrance closed we'll be safe forever."

"You're crazy!" Charlie shouted.

"Don't call me that!" he yelled. "I am the only sane one left! The answer to our survival is right beneath our feet. It's the earth itself. Dirt will be our salvation. It will keep us safe until we learn how to fight them. And we will learn, and one day we'll show them. We'll show them all. This is a war, a war between our world and theirs. And the only way to win it is to… Ugh!"

Keys croaked as something flashed against the back of his head. He reached up to touch the bump rising there, then his knees buckled and he slumped to the floor. The door swung wider open, revealing Martin, swaying on one foot, holding the crutch he had used as a club.

"Are you all right?" he asked.

Andy ran to his dad and hugged him so tight they both almost fell over.

Been'Tok realized the Great Warrior was no warrior at all, great or otherwise. He was a child. The strangely flat images An'Dee showed him proved it. Mar'Tin was not a servant, but the biped version of the nanny-bots that had raised Been'Tok. In the biped language, nanny-bots are called *Fa'Ther*.

Been'Tok felt like an idiot. How could he have thought a creature no taller than himself was a Warrior? In his defense, An'Dee had done many remarkable things. He had escaped the Seeker no less than three times, freed other bipeds from captivity, and daringly taunted a large wild beast.

What had Been'Tok done in his entire life that compared to what the child An'Dee had done since they landed beside his dwelling? He had obeyed the Masters' orders without question. He had cowered at the slightest glance of a Guardian. He was a Worker and that is what Workers did.

That was his past and no doubt his future once he returned to the Masters' ship. He would leave soon. Of the two damaged Seekers, one was broken beyond repair, but the other merely needed a new leg. The Grabbers were already hard at work salvaging a leg from the broken machine and fixing it into place.

The thought of returning to his dull labor filled Been'Tok with dread. And there was another feeling. He felt it when the Tarak'Nor ordered him to vaporize the lichen-covered stone on the red planet, only now the hollow emotion was a thousand times worse.

CHAPTER TWENTY-NINE

The Underground City

"He said we had to hide underground," Andy whispered, sipping cocoa. "He said we would have to hide here for years, maybe decades. That life wasn't about living anymore. Just surviving."

They all sat a table in the commissary, Hector and Charlie beside him and his dad straight across. The color had returned to Martin's cheeks, but he was still weak and rested his bandaged leg on a chair.

"That man was having a bad day," Martin said, digging into a plate of French toast and sausage. "Sometimes when a person goes through a terrible experience, it affects how they think."

"That's what Charlie said," Andy nodded.

"He was traumatized," she added.

"He was crazy," Hector said. "He wanted to blow us up."

"That isn't going to happen. He's not going anywhere."

They had dragged the unconscious Keys to the infirmary,

strapped his wrists and ankles to a gurney, and put a cold compress on his bruised head. He regained consciousness, but only after Martin removed the wires from the explosives and locked the trigger device away. The ring of keys now sat on the table before them beside the salt and pepper shakers and napkin dispenser.

"What now?" Charlie asked. "I want to find my mom."

"We need to know what happened," Andy said. "We need to find out where everyone was taken."

Martin pushed his plate away and tapped the ring of keys, "Let's go exploring."

Everyone brightened at the prospect. Limping on crutches, Martin led the way through the halls of the underground base. They found store-rooms, supply closets, and offices with desks piled high with papers. Down a flight of stairs were mechanical facilities, meeting rooms, and a chamber full of noisy generators. Another level down revealed sleeping barracks and a game room with pool tables, fitness machines, and a two-lane bowling alley.

It's a city, Andy thought. *An underground city.*

Keys had been right about one thing; they could live here for decades. Pine Mountain was designed to support its underground residents with all the comforts they had known on the surface. There was even a small grocery store, a barber shop, and a movie theater. The more Andy saw, however, the lonelier he felt, dwarfed in facilities designed for people now taken captive by the aliens.

Their search stopped at a large metal door marked COM-
MAND CENTER in crisp brass letters. The importance of
the room was clear from special locks that secured it. Martin
tried a dozen different keys before finding the right one. The
dark chamber beyond reminded Andy of NASA's mission
control, with tiers of computer stations descending to a wall
of monitors, their screens silent and black.

Stepping further into the room, Andy noted jackets and
sweaters hanging on the backs of chairs, half-filled cups of
coffee, and a forlorn donut with one bite taken out. It was
just like Charlie said, people had left suddenly to greet the
returning survivors when the aliens attacked.

"Look," Charlie said, pointing to one workstation. "That
computer is working."

They gathered around the computer screen and stared at
the small cursor flashing in one corner, savoring the hint
of civilization it represented. The computer was unlike anything Andy had seen before. The keyboard was enormous,
with dozens of strangely marked buttons in addition to the
traditional letters and numbers.

Charlie, undaunted, sat before the computer. She laced
her fingers, cracked her knuckles, then tapped out various
key combinations, her face pinched in concentration. She
typed LOGIN and hit return. Nothing happened. She tried
SYSTEM REBOOT, but still nothing happened.

Hector sat in a nearby chair and started spinning around
and around. "Can you operate that thing?" he asked.

"A little," she replied. "I watched my mom work on computers all the time. She taught me the basics."

"Listen," Martin said. "You hear something?"

Charlie stopped typing and Hector stopped spinning. In the stillness of the room they felt more than heard the distance booms.

"Oh, no," Hector mumbled.

Martin hobbled to the door. "All of you stay here."

"I'm going with you," Andy said.

He followed his dad back into the main corridor where the deep vibrations were louder. As they passed the infirmary, Keys struggled at his restraints and yelled, "What did I tell you? I told you they'd come back!"

Andy and Martin passed into the cavernous armory. The tripod steps shook the whole room and veils of dust descended from the ceiling. They cautiously approached the blast doors and peered out the lowest opening. Outside a lone tripod, dented and blackened from battle, marched back and forth. The machine stopped and faced them. Been'Tok waved from the machine's belly turret.

"It's just Been'Tok," Andy sighed. "Don't worry, Dad. He won't hurt us."

As though to prove the point, the machine stepped to the blast doors and crouched. Been'Tok hopped out of the turret and ambled forward. He stopped before the blast doors. Andy motioned for the alien to join them, but Been'Tok remained beside the tripod.

"An'Dee," the alien croaked, then added, "Fa'Ther."

"What's wrong?" Andy asked. "Why isn't he coming in?"

"I think he's leaving," Martin replied.

"Leaving? But we need him. Been'Tok, you can't leave."

"We can't stop him, son."

It had never occurred to Andy that the alien would leave. He had lost so much in the last few days; his family, his house, every neighbor on Otter Lane, and the entire town of West Bend. One of the only things he had gained was the friendship of the strange furry creature before him, and now it seemed he would lose that as well.

"Andy! Mr. McBean!" Hector called, running across the armory. He skidding to a halt beside them. "She did it! The computers, they're working. You gotta see this. It's crazy!"

"C'mon," Martin said.

Andy followed, but paused to wave for Been'Tok to join them. The alien turned from the tripod to Andy as though deciding between the two, then followed Andy across the armory and down the corridor to the Command Center.

The room was no longer dark and dead, but glowed with activity. The large monitors covering one wall vibrated with fat pixels of color. Hector pointed to one screen where digital static revealed a man wearing a bright blue turban. His lips moved, but the speakers only crackled with noise.

"Why can't we hear him?" Andy asked. "What's that on his head?"

"It's a turban," Charlie said.

"I recognize the flag behind him," Martin added. "I think he's Pakistani."

Andy waved at the screen and much to everyone's amazement, the man waved back. He seemed to be looking right through the monitor and into the room.

"Keep waving, Andy," Martin said. "There must be a camera here somewhere. Charlie, look for a volume control."

Charlie worked the keyboard before her, and the images on the screens grew larger, then smaller, then shifted from one monitor to another. Finally, a speaker came to life with a burst of feedback.

"… in Lahore, do you read me?" the man said.

"Hello, can you hear us?" Martin asked.

"I can't hear you," the man replied. "Can you hear me? This is Captain Pradesh in Lahore, Pakistan. Please identify yourselves."

Andy spied a pair of earphones dangling beside one workstation. They were just like the headphones he used to play video games and he fastened them over his head and positioned the microphone before his mouth.

"Hello?" he said.

"Who is this?" the man asked.

"This is Andy McBean."

"Andy McBean? What is your rank, McBean?"

"I'm in sixth grade."

"Sixth grade?"

"Yeah, you should probably talk to my dad."

"Your… dad?"

Andy tugged off the headset and handed it to Martin, who held the little microphone before his mouth. "Captain, this is Martin McBean. We are civilians at the Pine Mountain Army Base outside Port Cascade."

"Pine Mountain? We thought you were lost."

"The base was being used as refugee center, but the aliens attacked," Martin explained. "We're the only ones here. Can you tell us what's going on?"

Pradesh leaned forward, his face filling the monitor. "The situation is not good. The aliens have shut down all power networks across the planet. Local generators work and we still have direct satellite links, but they're spotty. My God, what is that behind you!"

Everyone faced Been'Tok, who in turn rotated his head to look behind him.

"Don't worry," Andy said. "He's with us."

Pradesh stared at the alien, dumbfounded. He scratched his dark black beard, then said, "I must report this. Please stand by."

Before Martin could say anything, the Pakistani touched the keyboard before him and his image vanished.

CHAPTER THIRTY

The Command Center

"**W**here'd he go?" Hector shouted. "What the heck! Where'd he go?"

"Calm down," Martin said.

Every monitor burst to life, filling the Command Center with a cacophony of color and sound. Faces filled every screen. Military personnel from around the world stared down on them, all talking at once. They pointed at Been'Tok, their questions tumbling out in a variety of languages and accents.

"Who are zey?"

"Can you talk with it?"

"Vhat do they vant?"

"Why did eet come here?"

"It might be a spy!"

"What are they building?"

"Vhat's dat machine on its shoulders?"

"It could be spying on us right now."

"Eez zat a weapon?"

"What is their technology?"

"Does it speak?"

"Are those eyes? Three eyes?"

"We should dissect it. See what makes it tick."

"Hey!" Andy shouted, not liking that idea at all.

"We need to know what they're building."

"And vy zay collecting all of da people."

"Listen…" Andy started, but the officers ignored him.

"Are there others coming?"

"Is this just the beginning?"

Andy took the microphone from his dad and held it close to his mouth. "HEY!"

The monitors squealed with a burst of feedback. The officers grimaced and rubbed their ears, falling silent.

"Its name is Been'Tok," Andy explained. "He does speak, but so far I've only learned that he's very fond of flowers. He saved my life and my dad's life, so we're not going to dissect him. Gross. As far as why they're here, I think it's because of the water. They want our water."

"My son is right," Martin added. "We passed a lake on our way here that was totally drained. Like they vacuumed up the water until it was bone dry."

The officers nodded and murmured among themselves. Some consulted with others off screen, passing papers back and forth, or pushing buttons on their computer keyboards. A few monitors filled with maps and charts. Everyone seemed to be talking at once. Andy wondered how any of them could make heads or tails out of anything being said.

A Chinese man and woman, both in military uniforms, filled one screen. The woman was young, her pretty eyes filled with youthful energy, but the man was older, his hair flecked with gray. He grimaced and said something in Chinese.

The pretty woman translated, "Your assumption sounds plausible. It follows that they would land in your region, which is one of the rainiest parts of the planet. Our satellites reveal they have set up some sort of base in Port Cascade and drained the reservoir in Center Park."

One screen shifted to a satellite image of Port Cascade. Andy recognized the tall buildings, the piers along the waterfront, and the green wedge of Center Park. A bright glow hovered over the trees. It was the same bands of light that had surrounded the alien cages, but here they enveloped the entire park. Beneath them an immense crowd covered the lawns and play fields like a shimmering fabric. Tripods passed back and forth through the shield, depositing their latest captives inside.

"It's a giant cage," he said. "They've turned Center Park into a giant cage."

The image shifted to the lake-sized reservoir in the center of the park. It was completely dry, drained right down to its concrete lining. Filling the empty bowl were two alien machines. One was shaped like a squat onion and rested on three landing pads. Metal plates covered its hull. At the very peak of the ship, a bright light emitted the green bands of the shield.

The other machine was still under construction. It was the shape of a giant egg, with a large opening on one side. Aliens swarmed over its skeleton, carrying parts and fitting them into place. Andy stepped closer to the monitor and studied the half-built machine. There was something familiar about it.

"I've seen this before," he said softly.

An American Colonel cleared her throat. "This is Colonel Tasker with Strategic Air Command. I can confirm they are building some kind of machine in Center Park."

"What is it?" asked the officer from Brazil. "A weapon? What are they planning?"

"Vee must destroy it!" shouted a general from Russia, slamming his fist against the table.

"We've tried," Tasker said. "It can't be done. Those moving lights are some sort of shield. We've sent in jets, their missiles all exploded when they hit those lights."

To prove the point, her image was replaced by another satellite view of Port Cascade. A trio of fighter planes soared over the skyscrapers toward the park. Missiles shot from beneath their wings, trailing smoke, then exploded against the glowing shield. For a moment the image was obscured in flames and smoke, but when the cloud dissipated, the shield remained as did the alien machines beneath it.

"That's it!" Andy shouted, breaking the silence.

"What's it?" asked the General from Nairobi. "What is that boy saying?"

"Eez he talking viz du alien?"

"Ask him what they're building!"

Andy pulled Been'Tok forward so every monitor could see them. He pointed to the projector in the middle of the breathing harness.

"Been'Tok," Andy said, "show them father."

The alien's eyes grew wide with understanding. With a swipe of his broad hand, the projector came to life emitting a swirling cloud of lights. The officers reacted with amazement and wonder.

The admiral from France cleared his throat. "What eez zat? Eez zat a veapon?"

Andy rolled his eyes. "Calm down. It's a photo album."

The hologram formed, revealing Been'Tok in his youth, cradled in the arms of a machine. Andy made a swiping motion in the air and Been'Tok shuffling through the three-dimensional images. Everyone watched, captivated, as each hologram revealed some new technological wonder or strange alien landscape.

Finally, Andy saw what he was looking for. "That's it, stop there. Look in the background. That's where I've seen the machine before. That's what they're building."

The hologram showed Been'Tok on a strange planet, lush with orange and blue plants. Far behind him, a large machine identical to the one under construction in Center

Park stood upon the banks of a purple lake fed by a pink waterfall. Strange birds with green wings flew around it.

Been'Tok swiped a hand across the image and the dots of light swirled as though caught in a brisk wind. They reformed into a larger image of the machine with the dark portal, several stories tall.

The image vibrated to life.

A swirling vortex formed around the portal. Wind rushed in, stripping trees of their branches and pulling trunks out of the dirt. The purple lake frothed and foamed. The pink waterfall turned to mist. The giant device sucked in clouds of vapor and when they finally dissipated, only the machine remained. The landscape was stripped bare, the trees and vegetation gone, the lake no more than a dusty depression.

Been'Tok shut off the projector. The officers stared grimly, their faces lined with sober resignation. Everyone knew that Port Cascade and perhaps the entire planet was destined for the same fate once the alien machine was finished and activated.

Captain Pradesh broke the silence. "It's some kind of evaporation machine. It extracts water from everything around it."

"We have to destroy it," said the admiral from the United Kingdom. "But how?"

The words tumbled out of the officers like an avalanche. Some pounded on the tables. Others waved and pointed.

"We must bomb them."

"We've tried that. It's hopeless."

"Use larger bombs."

"Nothing can get through that shield."

"Zere are people in zat park. Vould you kill zem?"

"That explains why they are rounding everyone up. Human beings are sixty percent water."

"We must do something or they will turn the earth into a desert."

"Port Cascade is just the start. Any of us could be next."

Andy slumped into a chair as the officers argued. What could be done? What weapon could stop the alien machine from sucking every drop of water from the earth? He thought of Duck Lake. Would the whole planet be turned into a dusty pit? He had always hated the rain, never realizing how important it was. He thought of his mom and Freddie, no doubt trapped in Center Park with the rest of the mob. He wanted to save them, but only the alien tripods could pass through the glowing shield as they entered and exited the reservoir.

"That's it," he whispered to himself. "I know what we have to do."

Been'Tok wondered if the gray and glowering faces before him were the true leaders of the bipeds. Their images stared down, much like the holograms of the Masters, only flat and contained in square frames. Judging from the size of their heads, they were giants, far bigger than An'Dee or Fa'Ther.

An'Dee seemed eager to show these biped giants the images of other worlds Been'Tok had visited. He had a variety to choose from, taken on numerous planets, but An'Dee was particularly interested in one showing the Vaporator. The enormous machine was undeniably impressive, and Been'Tok was eager to demonstrate its abilities. The display, however, drew only silence.

Perhaps the bipeds finally realized what was in store for their world. The Vaporator was almost finished. Soon the Masters would activate it and reduce every living thing in the region to moisture. The liquid molecules would be compressed and refined, then sent to the nearest tanker to be transported back to the home world. The process would repeat, over and over again, until the blue wet planet was a dry husk.

The new empty feeling returned as Been'Tok stared at the image of the Vaporator under construction. Dozens of Workers labored over the machine's frame. No doubt Been'Tok would have to join them as soon as he returned to the Master's ship.

An'Dee kept pointing to an image of the Masters' ship and the shield generator glowing at the top. The child then pointed to the Seekers passing back and forth through the shield. It was difficult to interpret An'Dee's motions, but his impersonation of a Seeker's lumbering walk was clear, and when he made the screaming sound of the ray gun, Been'Tok knew exactly what he had in mind.

Was An'Dee serious? Did he know how dangerous his plan was? The risk involved? And using the Seeker's weapon to destroy the shield would mean betraying Been'Tok's entire way of life.

The alien could hardly wait to get started.

CHAPTER THIRTY-ONE

An Even Crazier Idea

"You're making a terrible mistake," Keys said. Andy ignored him and carried an armful of blankets into the tripod. Been'Tok had parked the machine right in front of the blast doors. With the entry ramp lowered to the pavement it was easy to carry supplies right into the cabin. Charlie and Hector followed, arms full of freeze-dried food packs and bottles of water. Martin, still hobbling on crutches, carried a portable satellite phone.

Keys stood just inside Big Bertha, unwilling to even set foot into the light of day. "Listen to me. Staying here is the only safe choice."

"Maybe safe for you," Martin replied. "But not for the people in Port Cascade."

"They're lost," Keys said. "It's terrible, but they are lost. And you will be too if you try to help them."

"They are not lost," Charlie said from the top of the ramp. "They're alive and we're going to save them. We have a plan."

"Plan, hah! You don't even know if you can shut that shield gizmo down."

"Andy turned off the shield gizmos in every cage in West Bend," Hector said.

"Those are…. It's just…. This isn't some little cage. It's the whole park!"

"Been'Tok says it can be shut down, and I believe him," Andy said. "One blast from this machine's ray gun should blow that shield to smithereens. Then the fighter jets can fly in and blow up that giant machine."

"Only if you can get inside the shield," Keys shot back, eyes blazing. "And just how do you plan to get inside?"

Martin tapped the tripod with one of his crutches. "We will march right in like every other tripod."

Keys threw up his hands and shook his head. "You're… it… I can't… You're putting your lives in that creature's hands. How do you know it will betray its own kind?"

"We don't," Andy replied. "But I trust him. I can't explain why, but I trust him. He saved my life."

"And mine," Martin added.

"It's one thing to throw your life away, Martin. But think of the kids. Shouldn't they have a choice?"

Martin nodded. "You're right. Andy, Hector, Charlie, would you like to stay here with Keys?"

"No."

"Uh-uh."

"Charlie?" Martin asked.

She stepped off the ramp and approached the blast doors. "I think you should come with us, Keys. I know you're scared. I am too. We all are. And you've been through something terrible. But hiding off by yourself isn't the answer."

Andy thought she was crazy. The last thing he wanted was for Keys to join them, but Charlie held out her hand and it seemed, for a moment, that Keys might take it. Then he shook his head and stepped further back inside.

"Have it your way," he said. "But you'll see. Soon you'll see that I was right. The only answer is to hide."

Martin tossed the ring of keys to him. "Here, knock yourself out."

Keys fixed the ring back onto his belt and stepped deeper into the shadows, his voice echoing off the walls of the armory. "You'll all see. You'll go out there and you'll be surrounded by those things and then you'll know you should have listened to Keys. But I won't let you back in. I'll blow up Big Bertha and no one will ever get in again. It will be too late for you. For all of you!"

Charlie shook her head and walked up the ramp, passing Andy.

"What was that all about?" he asked.

"None of your business," she replied.

Andy carried the last load of supplies up the ramp. Martin limped in behind him. The interior of the machine was as strange as the exterior. Curved walls, struts, and beams seem to grow right out of the floor. The front wall was dominated by the large porthole. The control station rising before it had large buttons and dials. Other control stations lined the side walls, each with a chair shaped like a sling. Everything had been designed for creatures with three short legs and hands the size of frying pans.

Martin settled into one sling and placed the satellite phone upon the console. As he fixed the headset over his ears, the device came to life, a mosaic of faces on its small screen.

"Can you hear me, Captain Pradesh?" Martin asked.

The Pakistani Captain waved. "Yes, I hear you, McBean."

"We're starting out now. We should reach Port Cascade by early tomorrow morning. I'll check in every four hours until we do. Colonel Tasker, are your planes ready?"

"Our fighters will be standing by," Tasker replied, "ready to attack once the shield is down. Good luck, McBean."

Martin turned off the phone and gave Been'Tok a nod. The alien settled into the sling before the central console. A shower of sparks rose from it and assembled into a holographic map of the tripod and surrounding landscape. The alien moved one hand through the hologram and the entry ramp folded up and the hatch closed.

The machine swayed to life.

Everyone steadied themselves as the floor shifted. Hector dropped to one knee. Charlie grabbed hold of a structural beam. Andy held onto the console, feeling queasy as the view out the large porthole fell away.

The machine rose higher and higher. Been'Tok turned the

cabin away from the damaged blast doors and directed it across the charred battlefield that surrounded the base. Deep crunching vibrations resonated as they marched toward the steep hillside that dropped into the valley.

No, Andy thought. *It's too steep.*

He clung to the console with both hands and shut his eyes, anticipating a fall, but it never came. He opened one eye, then the other. The hologram showed the tripod marching down the slope, its three legs adjusting to the incline in such a manner that kept the cabin perfectly level.

Andy let go of the beam, shrugged, and smiled. "Having three legs is pretty handy in some situations."

"Nice ride," Hector said. "Like my uncle's Buick."

They all gathered around Been'Tok, who leaned back in his sling. Andy stepped to the porthole. The tripod swayed among the treetops. An eagle stirred from its nest as they passed. The world seemed different from such a height, and all the problems below somehow smaller. Andy felt a hand on his shoulder.

"How you doing?" Martin asked. "Nervous?"

"We're marching in an alien tripod to their mother ship, so yeah, I'm nervous."

"C'mon, I want to show you something."

He led Andy to the back of the cabin. Behind a curved beam, a small platform was recessed into the wall. Martin stepped upon it and pulled Andy beside him. He pushed a large button on the wall and the platform rose. A panel in the ceiling parted, revealing a deep blue sky and scattered clouds. They rose halfway through the opening before the platform stopped. The alien ray-gun swayed above them and a crisp wind filled their lungs with the scent of the forest.

"I found this hatch when we were loading the supplies," Martin said. "They must use it to make repairs, or clean stuff, or maybe just to enjoy the view."

The sun had begun its descent behind the western ridge. The mountains to the north formed a jagged tear against the evening sky. Straight ahead, the first stars reflected off the tripod's hull in such a way that it seemed the machine was marching through space itself.

"Pretty," Andy noted.

"I was thinking," Martin began. "Keys is right about one thing — this is a risky plan. It's dangerous and might not work."

"I know."

"When you were in the hospital and things didn't look good. I promised that if you got better, I'd do everything I could to protect you."

"I did get better," Andy said, "but you can't protect me from everything."

"I could drop you and the others back at the Bed and Breakfast. You'd be safe there. Plenty to eat."

Andy thought a moment, then shook his head. "Then I'd be no better than Keys. Hiding underground like a rat."

"I suppose not."

"You can't hide from the bad stuff, Dad. Bullies, bears, or aliens from another planet."

"Or your son getting leukemia," Martin added.

Andy nodded, realizing for the first time his cancer had not just happened to him, but his entire family. "Yeah, bad things happens whether you like it or not. Sometimes they crash-land right in your front yard."

A muffled blast echoed through the valley. They looked back up the hill and saw a plume of dust rise into the sky.

"I guess Keys finally locked Big Bertha," Martin said.

They faced away from the rising cloud. The landscape ahead spread before them as the lumbering tripod crunched its way down the valley and on toward Port Cascade.

CHAPTER THIRTY-TWO

Port Cascade

"Andy, wake up," Hector said, "We're getting close."
Andy's eyes fluttered open as Hector dashed back to the front of the tripod. Andy sat up from his make-shift bed on the floor and worked the cricks from his neck. The first light of dawn filled the room and the crunching drumbeat of the tripod's steps reverberated like a clock ticking down to midnight.

It was chilly. Andy wondered if alien tripods had central heating. Holding the blanket around his shoulders, he made his way forward. Been'Tok sat at the center console as he had been all night, the holographic map floating before him. Didn't aliens ever sleep?

Andy waved as he passed. "Good morning, Been'Tok."

The alien replied with a string of short words, but the only one Andy recognized was his own name. He joined the others at the window. Leaning against the frame, he could see what had attracted everyone's attention.

They had reached Port Cascade's industrial district. The tripod crunched its way down a wide boulevard, lined on either side with small warehouses and auto-repair shops. A stray dog, skinny and shivering in the morning cold, took one look at the approaching machine and cowered back into a small factory. Straight ahead, the skyscrapers of downtown rose across the shimmering waters of the harbor, lit from some unseen source.

Andy studied the towers, finding the tallest spire of the National Bank Building, and to its left the ornate Cascade Building. He knew that just to the north, hidden from view, was the Port Cascade Memorial Hospital.

"What is that glow in the city?" Hector asked.

"That's the shield over Center Park," Martin replied. "That's where we're going."

Martin's eyes were grim, but he smiled broadly. Andy knew that smiling even when you're nervous is a grown-up skill he had yet to master. He tried smiling back, but the effort was half-hearted and came to an abrupt end when Charlie gasped and Hector ducked to the floor.

Another machine appeared in the street ahead.

"Stay calm," Martin said. "We're just another tripod to them. Part of the family."

The approaching contraption was shorter and more com-pact, with no cabin for an alien crew. It carried a cage upon its numerous legs. Slender tentacles felt along the street, seek-ing people to join those it had already captured. It paused as the larger tripod marched by, then continued its search.

"See? I told you it would be fine," Martin smiled, then wiped beads of sweat from his forehead.

The tripod marched toward the port on the near side of the bay. Acre after acre was filled with stacks of metal cargo containers and the forklifts, rail cars, and eighteen-wheel trucks that carried them across the country. Towering overhead, cargo cranes dwarfed the tripod. Andy wished they could come to life on their metal legs and fight the alien machines in a mechanical death-match.

As the tripod approached the water's edge, he assumed Been'Tok would take them around the bay along the shore, but the tripod marched straight at the water.

"Been'Tok?" Andy asked.

"What's he doing?" Hector gasped.

"Hang on!" Martin said.

The entire cabin tilted as the tripod stepped off the pier and into the bay. Two more steps brought the water to the base of the cabin. Hector backed away as waves sloshed against the porthole. Soon they were underwater, the rippling surface rising above them, filling the cabin with dancing light.

"It's okay," Andy said, reassuring himself more than anyone else. "After all, the tripod has been in space. I guess going underwater is no big deal."

Charlie nodded, stepping closer to the window. Hector kept his distance as the tripod descended into the depths of the harbor, the daylight from above growing dim. With

Soon they were underwater, the rippling surface rising above them,
filling the cabin with dancing light.

a twist of his hand, Been'Tok activated the machine's searchlights and they cut beams through the murky water, revealing a new world.

Rocks and barnacle-crusted boulders littered the sea floor. Off to the left, the ribs of an ancient ship were now home to mussels, clams, and urchins of every kind. Swarms of tiny fish moved like flocks of birds, while larger fish darted around them, looking for their next meal.

Squeals and whistles echoed through the cabin. Andy peered into the darkness, searching for the source of the underwater music. His eyes grew wide as a trio of black and white Orca whales glided by, lit up by the tripod's lights. Andy waved to them and was greeted by a chorus of chirps. He forgot about the aliens that had invaded his planet, the evaporation machine they were building, and the urgent need to destroy the shield that protected it.

"I always hated the water," he said. "So... wet. I wonder if fish and whales feel the same way about the air."

"So... dry," Charlie smiled.

"Yeah. Guess it all depends on how you look at things."

The sea floor rose before them and the cabin was again filled with daylight. Andy vowed that if he survived the challenges ahead, he would learn more about this undersea realm and never again take it for granted.

The cabin broke through the surface. Sheets of water rippled across the porthole. The waterfront of Port Cascade lay straight ahead. With a lurching stride, the tripod stepped out of the bay and onto the old amusement pier. The whirligig and Ferris wheel shook as the machine lumbered across the thick wooden planks, but there were no people on the boardwalk, and no children on the merry-go-round.

Andy could hardly imagine a sadder sight than an empty amusement park, but the city was equally lifeless. The sidewalks were empty and no one leaned out the windows of the majestic Bayside Hotel to take in the view. The tripod stepped onto Waterfront Drive where abandoned cars lined the boulevard.

The city was dead.

"It's empty," Hector said. "Where'd everyone go?"

The only signs of life were stray dogs and more alien machines in a variety of shapes and sizes. In addition to other tripods, smaller machines scampered in and out of storefronts. One contraption, with more legs than Andy could count, crawled right up the side of a building and jabbed a silver tentacle into a window. It emerged a moment later clutching a screaming woman.

"They can climb," Charlie whispered. "I didn't know they could climb."

"I didn't know they could swim," Andy replied.

Martin turned on the satellite phone. He fit the headset over his ears and addressed the mosaic of faces on the small screen. "Everyone, we've made it to the city and are approaching the park."

"Good work, McBean," said Captain Pradesh.

"Our planes are holding position off the coast," said Colonel Tasker, her face breaking up with static. "As soon as the shield is down, they'll attack that machine."

"I understand," Martin nodded. "Your signal is breaking up. This may be our last transmission. I'm not sure the satellite uplink will work once we're inside the shield."

"Say again, McBean. Your transmission is weak."

"Hello?" Martin said. "Hello?"

There was no reply. The mosaic of faces froze and split into shifting squares of digital interference. Martin grimly removed the headset and set it aside.

Been'Tok guided the tripod down First Avenue and into the man-made canyons of downtown. The glow in the distance grew brighter with each crunching step. By the time the broad thoroughfare opened upon Center Park, the weaving bands of light were blinding. The park was filled with people. They sat on every bench and walkway and bike path. They crowded the Great Lawn, the ball fields, and soccer pitches. Some had even climbed the trees just budding with spring leaves. Andy looked for his mother's face, but knew it was futile. The throng stretched as far as he could see, and all were trapped behind the shield.

Charlie stared in rapt amazement. "I wonder if my mother is down there somewhere."

"And my family," said Hector.

"And my mom and Freddie," Andy added.

The tripod marched along the edge of the weaving lights.

More machines entered the boulevard from side streets, forming a strange alien parade, all heading toward the reservoir.

"What's happening?" Hector asked.

"They're all heading back to the main ship," Charlie noticed. "Maybe they're leaving."

"Or just taking cover," Martin said.

The alien ship rose several stories above the reservoir and the evaporation machine stood even higher. Massive tentacles lifted the final pieces of the device into place, completing the dark opening that dominated its face. Andy and the others marveled at the sight. In the holograms and satellite photos the machine had appeared small, almost like a toy, but rising before them, it was as imposing as any of the buildings surrounding the park.

The tripods just ahead stopped before the pulsating shield. One by one they passed into the empty reservoir. As their own tripod advanced in line, the shield seemed to move faster, setting the cabin ablaze with green light. Andy heard Been'Tok mutter and turned to offer a smile of encouragement. His face fell. Charlie and Hector gasped. Martin raised a crutch defensively.

Been'Tok aimed a glowing weapon straight at them.

CHAPTER THIRTY-THREE

Tricked

Been'Tok aimed the weapon menacingly at them. Hector raised his hands. Charlie followed suit, but Andy refused to budge, unwilling to believe he had been so mistaken about the alien's intentions. Had this all been a trap? A ruse to capture them?

"Been'Tok?" he asked.

The alien did not respond, but the projector on its harness glowed to life. A cloud of sparks assembled into an enormous alien head. It was the same Big Head hologram Andy had seen in West Bend. The giant alien barked commands in a booming voice. Been'Tok replied and pointed at his captives.

Martin pulled Charlie and Hector behind him, but Andy didn't budge. He was angry. Angry at being tricked, angry at coming this far only to be defeated, and angry that Keys may even now be laughing at their failure from deep inside Pine Mountain.

Andy stepped toward the holographic head and threw his fists through it, scattering the image into a billion dots. The image quickly reassembled and the Big Head shouted at Been'Tok. The smaller alien nodded and guided the tripod forward. Light flooded the cabin. Andy squinted at the glare. When he opened his eyes again, the light was gone. So was the Big Head.

And so was Been'Tok's weapon.

"Andy. Smile," the alien said.

"Huh?" Andy muttered.

Been'Tok's face moved with obvious strain. Seldom-used muscles pulled cheeks and lips in unfamiliar ways. All three eyes welled at the effort.

"What's he doing?" Hector asked.

Andy grinned, realizing, "He's... smiling."

A wide toothy smile spread across the alien's furry face. Flat teeth, one crooked, gleamed. Andy rushed forward and hugged Been'Tok, who croaked in surprise.

"What's happening?" Hector asked. "Will someone tell me what's happening?"

"The whole thing was a trick," Martin explained. "We're not his prisoners. He was just pretending to get us through the shield."

"Sneaky alien," Charlie added.

Been'Tok tousled Andy's hair and pointed to the tripod's holographic controls. They showed the machine walking along the running path that circled the reservoir. Smaller machines patrolled the area, keeping the mob of people away. In the reservoir, more aliens finished their work on the evaporation machine. Dozens ambled back to the alien ship, carrying tools and pushing equipment. A few larger Thugs shouted at them. Hovering over many were holographic Big Heads.

Andy studied the small aliens, noting the weary sadness in their eyes. How could aliens be sad? They had great ships and marching tripods. They could fly from one planet to another. With such tools, how could any of them be sad? And then it all became clear — he had read about it in history class.

"I know why Been'Tok's helping us," he said.

"Why, son?"

"Don't you see, Dad? He's a slave. Look at all the smaller aliens. They're doing all the work. The Big Heads give orders and the Thugs just push them around."

"Whatever the reason," Martin said, "we'll only get one shot at this. Once we blast that shield generator, those jet fighters will attack that machine."

Everyone gathered around the hologram floating above the center console. Martin reached inside the image and pointed to the tripod's weapon and then to the shield generator glowing atop the alien ship. Been'Tok nodded and guided the machine to a halt. Another swipe across the controls brought the ray gun to life. The cabin hummed with energy and the weapon took aim.

"This is it," Martin said. "Hang on."

Andy, Charlie, and Hector were already hanging on to whatever was handy. The noise of the ray-gun powering up reached a deafening crescendo... then died to silence.

The tripod lurched forward.

Andy fell to the floor. Charlie landed on top of him and both rolled into Hector. Martin cried out and toppled off his crutches. Even Been'Tok tumbled out of his sling, as confused as anyone by the sudden movement.

The cabin tilted violently, sending everyone rolling across the floor. Andy landed by the porthole. Outside, a large tentacle had wrapped itself around the legs of the tripod.

"What's happening?" Charlie shouted.

"A tentacle picked us up," Andy replied. "It's taking us to the ship."

CHAPTER THIRTY-FOUR

A New Plan

The tripod swayed like a boat on rough seas. Andy held onto the frame of the porthole and watched as the tentacle carrying the tripod lifted them across the hull of the ship toward a large opening.

"What happened?" Hector asked. "Did it work?"

Andy glanced up and saw the pinnacle of the vessel still glowed bright. Bands of light wove outward from the shield generator and stretched across the park.

"No," Andy replied. "The weapon never fired. The shield is still going."

"An'Dee," Been'Tok croaked.

Andy found the alien across the cabin, standing over Martin who lay sprawled on the floor.

"Dad!"

Andy scrambled to Martin's side and rolled him onto his back. A red scrape marked the spot where his forehead had hit the cabin wall.

"Is he okay?" Charlie asked.

"He hit his head. Get the first aid kit."

"Andy!" Hector yelled, pointing out the porthole. "Look!"

Outside, the large tentacle wrapped around the tripod was carrying them right inside the alien ship. The vast hangar was filled with dented and damaged machines of all shapes and sizes. On the floor below, scores of aliens worked on broken equipment, some with great welding devices strapped to their backs, others riding on smaller machines that lifted new parts into place or dragged broken ones away. Sparks flew and the chamber clanged with the racket of their work.

"It's a body shop," Andy yelled. "They must think we're broken and came back for repairs."

Charlie set the first aid kit beside Martin. She grabbed a chemical pack and worked it in her hands until it turned cold. Andy set the pack on Martin's bruised forehead and fastened it in place with a bandage.

"Grown-ups can sure take a beating," Charlie said.

The gentle sway of the cabin ended with a quick descent and a resounding thud. Everything rattled then fell quiet as the cabin came to a rest at a tilted angle. Andy glanced at the console. The hologram floating over it showed the tripod resting in a heap of broken equipment.

"They've set us down," Hector said. "What do we do now, Andy?"

"I don't know."

"What about the shield?" Charlie asked. "We have to shut it down. Can we shoot it from here?"

Andy studied the hologram again and shook his head. "No way. We'd have to shoot through the whole ship."

"What do we do? We have to shut it down."

"I'm thinking."

"It's over," Hector said. "That's it. It's over."

"It's not over!" Andy yelled. "I had cancer. I know what over looks like and this isn't it!"

"Andy..." Hector exclaimed, nodding to Charlie.

"Hector, who cares if Charlie knows that I was sick?"

"You had cancer?" Charlie asked.

Andy met her puzzled gaze. "I should have told you sooner, but I just... I was tired of being *the kid who had cancer*. I had leukemia. I was in the hospital a long time and almost died. My hair fell out and my hearing is still a bit fuzzy, but I'm better now. I'm sorry if that freaks you out or if you think I'm toxic or radioactive. And no, I didn't see a bright light, and I don't see dead people."

"My dad's in jail," Charlie blurted.

"Huh? Jail?"

Andy rubbed his ears to make sure they were working properly. "You're dad's in..."

"Jail. He was in the army and had problems when he came back from deployment," Charlie explained. "And he got in trouble and was arrested."

"But you said he lives in Seattle."

"He does, Andy. In the jail there. I guess I should have told you, but my mom thought if we moved here and made a fresh start I wouldn't be *the kid whose dad is in jail.*"

Andy was speechless. It all made sense now. Charlie's sobs in the bathroom. Her fear of being left alone. Her bragging about how great her dad was. And her sympathy for Keys and the trauma he'd been through.

"I play the clarinet," Hector offered, breaking the silence.

Charlie ignored him. "You're lucky, Andy. You got better, and you still have your dad."

Did she say he was lucky? That's crazy. Cancer is not the sort of thing that happens to lucky people and neither are alien invasions. And yet he had gotten better. And he had survived since the tripod stepped out of the meteor on his front lawn. More than survived, he had lived, evaded capture, helped his friends, and met new ones. Maybe he was lucky. Maybe he was no longer *cancer boy*, or never had been, and the only person he needed to convince of that was himself.

He stood beside the console and pointed to the hologram of the alien ship and the glowing shield at the top.

Charlie joined him. "What are you thinking, Andy?"

"If we can't destroy the shield from the outside, then we have to shut it down from the inside."

"Go outside the tripod?" Hector asked. "But there a thousand aliens out there."

Charlie picked up Been'Tok's weapon. "We could fight our way with this!"

"We'd never make it," Hector said.

Andy took the gun from Charlie. "No, not as fighters, but maybe as prisoners. Just like we got through the shield."

He handed the weapon to Been'Tok. The alien looked puzzled until Andy stepped back and raised his hands.

"I get it," Charlie said. "C'mon, Hector, stand up. Raise your hands."

"We just give up?"

"What about your dad?"

"We'll leave a note," Andy said, then added, "Been'Tok, take us to your leaders."

*

Moments later, Andy kneeled by his dad, adjusted the pillow under his head, pulled a blanket over his shoulders, and made sure the note he'd written was safe in his pocket. Satisfied, he nodded for Been'Tok to open the front hatch. The ramp crunched onto the discarded equipment below.

Charlie peered out the hatch. "Looks all clear."

Been'Tok led the way out of the tripod, weapon in hand, followed by Charlie and Hector. Andy brought up the rear. Once he was off the ramp, it folded closed and the hatch hissed shut.

Been'Tok led them toward a nearby doorway when a voice barked from behind. Hector yelped. Charlie grabbed Andy's arm.

A small alien, smudged and smeared with dirt and grease, appeared from around a scrap pile. It barked again. Been'Tok replied and gestured to his captives. A second alien ambled forward, then a third and a fourth. Soon Andy was surrounded by brown fur and large staring eyes. They were all workers, no taller than himself, and wore breathing harnesses, helmets, and tool-belts.

Been'Tok addressed them. The projector on his harness emitted a holographic image of Andy on his front porch, in his animal pajamas and moose-slippers. The aliens purred, clearly impressed, and backed away a few paces.

"Nice slippers," Charlie smirked.

Andy turned red as the doors behind him slid open, revealing a small chamber. Been'Tok led them inside. Only when the doors slid shut, blocking out the noise and crowd of the hangar, did everyone sigh in relief.

"What was that all about?" Hector asked.

"I don't know," Andy replied.

"I think they thought you were some kind of leader," Charlie said. "Now what?"

As though in reply, the room filled with a rushing wind blowing from every direction. The sound filled their ears, drowning out their shouts of surprise. The blast whipped their hair and pushed their faces into strange shapes.

When the torrent subsided, the wall opposite the door opened, revealing a curtain of rippling light. Everyone shielded their eyes from the glare, but Been'Tok nudged

Andy into the bright veil. The air within smelled sweet and clean. His skin tingled and his hair stood on end. He felt different, as though he were floating.

Andy stepped out of the waves of light and into the vast interior of the alien ship. Floors, walls, and ceilings reached several stories high. The tall atrium reminded him of the Port Cascade Shopping Mall, with levels rising on either side, connected here and there with bridges. Aliens passed on every floor. Several stopped to stare, snapping holograms with the metallic harnesses they all wore.

The veil of light parted behind him as Hector and Charlie emerged. Andy could tell by their expressions that they also felt the strange sensation. Charlie's long hair floated and rippled as though she were underwater.

"I feel lighter," she whispered.

"Feels like my guts are floating inside," Hector added.

"I think the gravity is different in here," Andy replied and to prove the point, he jumped up and gently floated back to the floor.

"Uh-oh," Hector hissed.

He pointed at the two giant aliens lumbering toward them. They were Thugs, three times the height of Been'Tok and twice as wide. Muscles knotted their legs and arms, and both carried large weapons. The largest one stopped before them and bent over, its largest eye so close that Andy could see his reflection in the dark iris.

Been'Tok emerged from the wall of light, his weapon at

the ready. One Thug bellowed at him, but Been'Tok stood as tall as possible, waved to Andy, and barked a few words in reply. He pointed to the highest level of the ship where the outer walls of the atrium gathered together, then activated his holographic projector. The image of Andy in his colorful pajamas floated before them. Both Thugs backed up a step.

"See? They think you're a leader," Charlie whispered. "Stand tall. Try to look important."

Andy stood tall and held his head high. The Thugs stepped aside and Been'Tok led the group to a platform recessed into a nearby wall. They stepped upon it and the floor instantly began to rise. There was no railing and Hector nervously backed away from the edge.

"That was close," he said, "but I think it's working."

"They sure like your pajamas," Charlie smirked.

The platform slowed to a stop at the highest level of the atrium, before a broad set of windows. As they stepped off, a low rumble filled their ears.

"What's that noise?" Hector asked.

Charlie pointed out the windows. "Guys, check it out."

Outside, the evaporation machine on the far side of the reservoir hummed to life. Dust and vapor swirled into its dark portal. A flock of birds struggled to fly away, but their wings were no match for the machine's pull and they were quickly sucked inside.

"It's started," Andy said. "We're too late. They've started the machine."

CHAPTER THIRTY-FIVE

The Big Heads

B een'Tok pulled Andy from the window and pointed to a bridge some steps away. It spanned the atrium and led to an ornate portal guarded by two giant Thugs. They were the biggest aliens Andy had seen. Each carried a weapon, but only wore a bright yellow sash over their dark fur.

Andy gulped, raised his hands over his head, and started across the bridge. Charlie and Hector followed, hands also raised, with Been'Tok trailing behind. The short alien put on a good act, waving his weapon and prodding them with sharp words that probably meant something like, *Get moving, human scum.*

They stopped at the far side of the bridge. The giant Thugs approached and barked at Been'Tok who shivered with dread. Charlie nudged him with her elbow, and the smaller alien stammered a reply, then showed the hologram of Andy. The Thugs were not impressed with Andy, his pajamas, or his moose-head slippers, but waved the portal open and Been'Tok quickly pushed his captives into the circular room beyond.

Workstations lined the walls. Holographic controls floated above each station, depicting the ship's engines, tentacles, life support systems, and even the evaporation machine. The small aliens before each console glanced their way, but soon returned to their chores.

"We made it," Hector gulped. "Now let's shut this thing down and get out of here."

"There it is," Charlie said, pointing to a hologram of the shield around the park.

"We need to find the off switch," Andy replied.

He pulled Been'Tok toward the shield hologram, but as they crossed the room, the ceiling opened directly over-head, bathing them in dazzling light. The section of floor on which they stood, lifted them through the opening and into a brilliant chamber of polished metal and glittering gems in every shade in the rainbow.

"Boy, I sure wish the floor in this ship would stay in one place," Hector gasped.

To the left, a large window offered a perfect view of the evaporation machine. The vortex swirling around its portal ripped leaves and branches from the nearest trees. To the right stood two more Thug aliens. Each wore yellow sashes and carried a weapon. Behind them rose a podium of gold, like the courtroom table judges would sit behind, only here the judges were five enormous aliens. Andy could only see their heads, each as tall as Been'Tok's entire body.

The Big Heads, Andy thought.

They feasted upon dishes of multicolored goo, their fat mouths sucking and slurping in great gulps. Goo dribbled off their lips and onto their furry chins. Hector gasped and backed away. Been'Tok cowered. Charlie gulped.

"Andy," she whispered. "It's them. The Big Heads. What do we do?"

Andy couldn't take his eyes off the enormous, terrifying creatures. No wonder the smaller aliens like Been'Tok trembled beneath their holograms. One of the Big Heads leaned forward and studied him with enormous eyes. Its deep voice filled the chamber with barking commands. Been'Tok stepped forward nervously, eyes pleading, and spoke softly. His projector glowed, showing the hologram of Andy in his pajamas, and other images of Andy riding in the back of the pickup, fleeing from the marauding tripod, opening the cages in West Bend, and running from the raging bear.

The Big Heads only glanced at the holograms, then returned to their gooey meal. One barked at the two Thugs, who stepped forward, their weapons aimed and glowing bright green. Andy backed away from the weapons, right to the wall of glass. He looked about the room for some exit or a place to hide, but there was none. It was over. Their mission had failed. They had come close, but they had failed.

Andy shook his head and looked out the large window. The swirling vortex around the evaporation machine had grown larger and more powerful. The mobs of people in Center Park ran from the lashing wind it created. Andy had to imagine their screams and cries. None of those sounds reached this guarded sanctum.

He wanted to yell at the injustice of it all. But a hard knot in his chest refused to give the Big Heads the satisfaction. As they continued their slurping feast, he looked out to Center Park and thought of the many days he had spent in the hospital, yearning to be healthy enough to run across its fields and breathe fresh air again.

The air.

Andy smiled and wondered if he wasn't indeed the luckiest person on the planet.

"Been'Tok," he said, "smile."

Hopeless. It was all so hopeless. The plan was simple enough and Been'Tok was particularly proud of his ruse to gain passage through the shield, but it had all gone awry when the big Grabber lifted the Seeker into the repair bay.

The sadness Been'Tok felt was tempered by the pride of trying. He had never tried anything so daring before. For a few moments he was more than a mere Worker, more than a recipient of orders, and a doer of tasks. What had changed him? What had made him think that among all the Workers he was somehow… something?

An'Dee had changed him. The biped never quit. Perhaps he was a Great Warrior after all. Even now he pointed out the window to the Vaporator and the swirling clouds of debris floating on the air.

The air.

CHAPTER THIRTY-SIX

Fresh Air

Andy raised his hands and pointed to the window behind him. Been'Tok's eyes grew wide with understanding.

"An'Dee smile," the alien croaked.

Andy whispered to Hector and Charlie, "Get ready to hit the deck."

"What? Why? What's going on?" Hector asked.

Been'Tok fired his weapon wide of Andy's head and into the window. The thick crystal shuddered and cracked. The second bolt of green energy sent jagged fissures across the entire porthole.

"Duck!" Andy yelled, dropping to the floor.

Charlie and Hector sprawled beside him. The Big Heads barked and growled. One Thug turned its weapon on Been'Tok, but as it was about to fire, the window exploded with a rush of pressurized air, pulling the weapon right out its hands.

Anything not tied down was sucked out the window. Been'Tok lost his own weapon. The bowls of colorful goop flew off the high table. Andy slid across the floor toward the opening, pulled by the rushing wind. He waved his arms, grasping for anything that could stop his slide.

Charlie grabbed hold of one hand and now both were pulled toward the shattered window. Been'Tok grabbed Charlie's legs, but his weight only slowed their progress. Andy slid over the ledge as the noise of the evaporation machine across the reservoir filled his ears. The dark vortex tugged at him like an invisible claw, pulling his legs further out the window. Terrified, he saw only the darkness trying to consume him, and the perilous drop down the ship's hull to the reservoir below.

The Big Heads behind the table bellowed, angry their meal had been splattered around the chamber. One Thug wiped goo from his face. The other bared its teeth and raged toward Been'Tok when a new sound pierced the din. A primal scream of pent up rage.

A banshee yell.

Hector rammed the large alien. The Thug yelped and staggered. It made a half-hearted swipe at Hector, who backed away, not out of fear, but to get a good running start. He rammed the Thug again, driving it toward the open window. The beast clutched the frame, eyes fluttering and lips quivering with a muffled growl.

It fell.

The tumbling alien left yellow smudges down the hull of the ship until it was caught by the vortex and sucked into the dark machine. The other Thug grabbed Hector, shaking him like a rag doll. Andy could only watch helplessly. It seemed his friend would be torn limb from limb when the Thug coughed, wretched, and loosened its grip. Hector wriggled free as the Thug dropped to one knee. The Big Heads watched, concerned, but by the time the Thug collapsed on the floor, they were also gasping for breath.

"Hector!" Charlie yelled.

Hector grabbed Andy's arms. With Been'Tok's help, they all pulled him back into the chamber where he kicked at the invisible claw until he was certain it had released him. They lay exhausted, catching their breath.

"What happened?" Hector asked. "Why did those Thugs pass out?"

Andy pointed to the vents on Been'Tok's respirator. "There's something in our air that makes them sick, remember? And the Thugs and Big Heads aren't wearing the harnesses like Been'Tok is."

"Smart move, but we still have to shut that machine down," Charlie said, pointing out the window.

A new sound filled the room. Deep growls rumbled from behind the high table. One giant alien face emerged to the left, another to the right. They were surrounded. Even Been'Tok shook with fear. The first Big Head staggered forward and for the first time they saw its entire body.

The Big Heads were not giants at all.

Their large heads rested atop small bodies with thin arms and legs. They lurched out from behind the high table, coughing and gagging. One slumped unconscious and another tried to pull it forward, but lacked the strength and also collapsed. The floor in the center of the chamber started to descend and the other Big Heads crawled to it, tumbling over the edge.

"C'mon," Andy yelled. "Jump!"

They leaped onto the platform and by the time it reached the control room below, the ceiling overhead had closed tight. Andy scrambled to his feet as the largest Big Head bellowed, its booming voice filling the room. It pointed at Andy and Been'Tok, but the smaller aliens stationed around the room just cowered. Andy wondered if they had ever seen the Big Heads in the flesh before. Perhaps the alien leaders were only known from the holograms of their giant heads, and not their spindly bodies.

One small alien stepped forward and the Big Heads backed away. It was just a step, probably an involuntary reaction, but told everyone they were afraid. The smaller alien growled and attacked, grappling the nearest Big Head to the floor. Others joined the fight, tackling the remaining Big Heads who yelped and cried as they were lost in a tangle of punches and kicks.

The portal to the control room slid open and two Thugs entered, shocked at the commotion before them. Before they could raise their weapons, however, they too were attacked by several smaller aliens.

"Andy, over here," Charlie shouted from across the room.

She stood before a hologram of the evaporation machine. Andy pulled Been'Tok toward it and pointed to the image.

"Shut it down," he said. "Turn it off."

Been'Tok swiped his hand through the hologram. The violent storm around its portal died to a gentle breeze and the tree trunks, park benches, ice cream carts, and anything else caught in its pull fell to the ground. Andy saw the hologram of the shield nearby, and pulled Been'Tok toward it.

"Now this one."

Been'Tok took hold of the holographic controls and the weaving bands of light quickly faded.

It was done. The shield was off.

Andy stepped to a nearby window to confirm the barrier over the park was indeed gone. Far below the mob of people had already begun to disperse, fleeing the park. Andy had been so fixated on shutting down the shield that he could hardly believe what his eyes told him to be true.

It was over. They had done it.

Charlie pointed at the alien melee and asked, "Andy, why are they fighting each other? What's happening? "

"Revolution," he replied.

CHAPTER THIRTY-SEVEN

Revolution

The ship rocked from a muffled explosion as jet fighters screamed overhead. Andy grabbed hold of the console before him and Charlie grabbed hold of Andy. "You hear that?" she asked.

"Even I can hear that," Andy replied. "The fighter planes are attacking."

Out the porthole, silver streaks flashed across the sky. The giant evaporation machine exploded with fire and smoke. Panels buckled and collapsed.

We did it, Andy thought, *we won.*

The device had been shut down, and judging from the repeated blasts of the jet fighters, it would never start again. The determination that drove Andy to his goal was suddenly replaced by the pain and weariness of the journey.

Hector pulled his arm. "Andy, let's get out of here!"

Black smoke puffed from vents on the walls. In the melee, Thugs grimaced, eyes fluttering as the smaller aliens beat them into submission. Been'Tok led the way around the fight. The ship rocked again as they left the control room and ran to the bridge spanning the atrium. On every level below, Thugs not equipped with air-filtering harnesses dropped to their knees and smaller aliens attacked, beating them to submission or vaporizing them with their own weapons.

"The big aliens are dropping like flies," Charlie noted.

Andy pointed to the smoking vents. "The air from outside is making them sick."

They leaped upon the platform as the chaos raged around them. Another explosion rattled the atrium. Windows shattered. Vents belched more black smoke. Hector lost his footing and almost fell off the platform. Fighting raged on every level they passed. Small aliens attacked gasping Thugs. Green bolts of energy cut through clouds of smoke. The scream of jet fighters roared overhead. A new round of explosions rattled the atrium. The platform lurched to a halt. Andy toppled upon Been'Tok. Hector fell on his rump. Charlie rolled toward the edge of the platform.

"Charlie!" Andy shouted, grabbing for her.

She tumbled over the side.

Andy crawled the edge, bracing for the worst, but Charlie floated just a few feet below, gradually descending in the ship's strange gravity.

"It's okay," she yelled. "C'mon, jump!"

Hector gulped. "Is she serious? Andy, I'm not jumping. No way. That's crazy."

"C'mon, Hector," Andy replied. "Time for that banshee yell again."

They clasped hands and leaped off the platform, Been'Tok close behind. The revolution raged, but Andy wasn't afraid. Why wasn't he afraid? He should be afraid. Then he remembered Paul and what he had said about getting better and being better. Andy smiled, understanding, as the gentle pull of the ship's gravity carried them to the atrium floor.

They landed.

Charlie was already standing before the wall of light that led to the hangar bay. Been'Tok pushed them through the tingling veil and into the airlock beyond. The door to the hangar opened, revealing a dozen expectant alien faces. Been'Tok spoke to them, quick and decisive. The furry crowd nodded and dispersed.

The ship lurched again, but this time it felt different. The floor swayed and a steady hum filled the cavernous chamber. Andy looked out the large opening of the hangar and saw Center Park tilt and sway.

"Oh, no," he gasped. "I think we're taking off! We need to get out of here!"

"Too bad," Charlie shot back. "I was just getting used to being light as a feather."

Andy had no desire to soar to into the heavens. His daydream of climbing into one of his model spaceships and finding a new planet was long gone. All he could think about was his father, his family, and his home in the wettest corner of the earth.

They ran to the tripod through the mounds of broken machinery. The ramp was already open and Martin stood at the bottom.

"Andy!" he yelled, waving a crutch.

"Dad," Andy shouted, running to him.

"What's happening?" Martin asked.

"We lowered the shield," Charlie replied. "The jets destroyed the machine, but it looks like this ship is leaving."

"Leaving?"

"As in the planet," Hector added. "We're taking off!"

Inside the tripod, Been'Tok pulled Andy to the main console and placed his hand flat upon it. The cool metal hummed to life. Andy felt a vibration course through his hand and up his arm. The weariness and exhaustion that had consumed him was chased away by a surge of energy. Been'Tok nodded out the porthole toward the opening of the hangar and the green trees outside.

"Andy," the alien said softly, nodding to the green vista.

Andy knew Been'Tok was right. This is where he belonged. This was his home, his city, and his planet. Andy smiled as the alien tapped the dented vent on his harness. Andy knew the gesture meant both *thank you* and *good-bye*. With a trembling smile, he hugged the alien tight. He felt Hector and Charlie join them, each hugging the alien and running their hands through its thick fur. Charlie even kissed Been'Tok's cheek, a gesture that set all three of its eyes fluttering. Andy felt a mixture of happiness and relief, laced with the awareness that he would never see his newest friend again. Been'Tok tousled his hair then ambled down the ramp, offering a last glimpse of fur as the hatch closed.

"Andy, what's going on?" Martin asked.

Where would you like to go, Andy?

"What?" Andy asked.

"I said what's going on?" Martin asked again.

"No, not you."

Where would you like to go?

Andy felt the vibration of the control panel reach his mind. It was the machine. The tripod was speaking to him. And it wasn't called a tripod. It was called a Seeker.

Andy, where do you want to go?

"I want to go out," Andy said.

"Who are you talking to?" Charlie asked.

"Out the opening," Andy replied. "Back to the surface."

Even before he finished speaking, the machine rose to its full height. Andy noted that large metals doors had begun closing across the opening of the hangar.

"Go outside," Andy said. "Before those doors close."

"Who's he's talking to?" Hector asked.

"Quiet," Andy snapped.

I don't think we will make it.

"Then run!" Andy yelled.

The cabin lurched forward as the Seeker ran across the repair bay. Charlie and Hector knelt on the floor. Martin settled into a nearby sling. The Seeker kicked aside broken machinery, equipment, and anything else in its path.

The doors are closing.

"Yes, I'm aware the doors are closing!" Andy shouted. "I can see them closing straight ahead of… whoa!"

The floor lurched and the view outside tilted so that only blue sky could be seen. The Seeker was running uphill now, struggling with every step.

"Run faster!" Andy shouted.

The doors continued to slide across the opening, shutting out the sky. The floor lurched again, this time forward. Hector and Charlie rolled to the front porthole. Now the tripod was running downhill.

"Jump!" Andy yelled.

The tripod jumped, springing on all three of its legs through the hangar doors. Everything floated weightless, then the Seeker landed with a deafening crunch, its legs absorbing the impact. Andy gripped the console, but his hands were no match for the force that threw him across the cabin into the back wall.

He landed upon Charlie and Hector in a pile. Once they untangled their legs and arms, they sat a moment, reassured at the stability of the machine beneath them. Andy wanted the entry hatch to open and as soon as the idea formed in his mind, the cabin descended and settled to the ground. The hatch opened, flooding the cabin with sunlight.

It read my thoughts, Andy realized. *The Seeker knows what*

I'm thinking.

Of course I do, Andy.

Andy helped his dad to the hatch and they all gathered on the ramp. Across the reservoir, the giant alien machine had collapsed. The dark vortex belched flame and smoke. High overhead, the alien ship receded into the sky.

Where the ship had stood, amidst pavement crushed by its landing pads, a group of Thugs and Big Heads writhed in agony. Without a respirators, they staggered sick, eyes glassy and drool dripping from their pale lips. One jumped into the air toward the ship that only rose higher away. A group of stray dogs circled, eyes hungry and teeth bared. A German Shepherd led the pack, biting one Thug's leg.

Andy turned away from the pathetic sight. He felt his father grip his shoulders. Charlie took hold of one hand and Hector the other and together they watched the alien ship grow smaller and smaller, until it was lost in the blue sky of a new day.

The blue planet receded into the darkness of space. Been'Tok was pleased that the damage they had inflicted upon it was minor. The planet should exist, he thought, just as the bipeds should keep their water, and Workers should have time to study pretty growing things.

The Masters were no more and would never again loom in holographic domination. The Guardians had been disarmed or thrown off the ship. The Workers went about their tasks, much as they always had, but with a new sense of... something.

Been'Tok made a note to invent a word for this new feeling. Perhaps he would call it *An'Dee* to honor the small biped who had saved his life in more ways than one. There was plenty of time now. Plenty of time to chart a new course and a new future. And plenty of time to invent the many new words they clearly needed.

EPILOGUE

A New World

With the shield shut down and the alien ship lost in the sky, the panic that had gripped Center Park turned to relief and, eventually, order. Police officers, firefighters, and national guard soldiers from Pine Mountain established first aid stations and organized search parties to gather food and supplies.

A lost and found was set up near the zoo, not for misplaced wallets and purses, but for misplaced people. Through the rest of the day and into the night friends met friends, wives found husbands, and children were reunited with parents. It was there that Martin registered their names and found a place to rest beneath a tree. It was there a woman with long black hair screamed, "Charlene!" and Charlie ran to her, tears streaming down her face.

Eventually, Charlie pulled her mom back to Andy and said, "Mom, this is Andy McBean. He saved my life twice. And then I saved his once."

An hour later Hector's parents shouted his name and swept him into their arms. Andy wondered when he would hear his own mom call to him. What would she say about his many cuts and scrapes? Would she send him to bed for a month, or see he was no longer the boy he used to be?

After hours of searching the crowd of people, Andy finally caught sight of Freddie's dishwater brown hair leaning against a woman's shoulders.

"Mom," he shouted.

His mom turned and searched the crowd, but her gaze passed right over him. He pushed his way toward her.

"Mom!" he shouted again.

She turned to the sound of his voice and their eyes met, Andy was sure of it, but his mom kept looking, her gaze darting from face to face. Didn't she recognize him? He elbowed his way toward her and grabbed her arm. She looked down, startled, a flicker of puzzlement on her face.

"Andy!" she shouted, dropping to her knees.

She hugged him, then held him at arms length as though checking that he was, indeed, her son. Apparently convinced, she hugged him again.

"Oh Andy," she said. "I hardly recognized you."

Andy led her to where Martin rested. One look at his face told Dara that he needed a doctor, and she took charge as all the best grown-ups do, with gentle persistence. Within an hour they were passing through the doors of the Port Cascade Memorial Hospital. It was the last place Andy wanted to go. He shuddered at the memory of his illness, the draining pain of treatment, and the feeling of being trapped forever inside the building's thick stone walls. The feelings made his knees weak and, suddenly exhausted, he slumped to the floor of the crowded waiting room, a forest of legs standing around him.

*

Andy woke the next morning in a room almost identical to the one he had shared with Paul in the Cancer Ward. For a moment he thought Paul was standing by his bed, but that was impossible. It was his mom, sleeping in a chair, and Freddie curled up in another.

"Hey, Andy," Freddie said.

"Hey, Freddie," Andy replied.

"Are you sick again?"

"No, I'm better now."

Andy considered calling to his mom, but she seemed peacefully asleep and it wouldn't be right to wake her. Across the room, Martin slept in another bed, his head bandaged and leg wrapped in a cast and elevated on wires. Charlie was right, grown-ups can sure take a beating.

With his family safe and together, Andy slept the deep sleep that only comes when all is right with the world. He dreamed of his adventures, now just a confusing jumble of recollections. He remembered the people who had helped him, including a furry alien who loves growing things. He thought of Paul, who had encouraged him every step of the way, or perhaps just reminded him of something he should have learned in these very walls. That hardships make you stronger, and you can not only get better from an illness, but because of it.

In the days to come, life back in West Bend returned to something that resembled normalcy. Greetings on Main Street were more heartfelt, handshakes firmer, and hugs tighter and held longer than customary. The wounded were treated, the dead buried, and stories of the invasion traded like baseball cards over cups of coffee at the B-Liner Diner and beers at the Lucky Nite Tavern.

Gradually word spread of how three kids had foiled the alien plot to take the earth's water. There were pats on the back from complete strangers for Andy, Charlie, and Hector. When Main Street had been cleared of rock and rubble, a ceremony was held in Founder's Park awarding each of them a Certificate of Thanks.

It was the first of many certificates, ribbons, and medals — one given to Andy by the Governor himself on the steps of the state capitol. His picture was taken and appeared on the front page of the Port Cascade Times under the headline, *Boy Saves Planet!* After the ceremony, one reporter asked, "How has this changed you?"

Andy thought for a moment, then replied, "I'm not sure yet. But my folks say I can play soccer again."

Andy was certain of one thing: the labels other people give you only mean something when you start to believe them. He was no longer *cancer boy*, any more than Hector was *clarinet girl*, Charlie *the kid who's dad is in jail*, or Been'Tok a *slave*.

Soon the world was ready to go about its business again, and Andy was ready to be just a boy again, but some things can be repaired more easily than others. The great trench on Otter Lane was filled, the shell of the landing vessel hauled away, and new rose bushes planted in the front yard. Andy stayed close as Martin inspected their damaged house. Repairs would require lumber, insulation, and plaster for the walls. Joists, plywood, and shingles for the roof. Hobbling on crutches through the remains of Andy's bedroom, Martin noted each item on a yellow pad. There was something about the orderly list that gave Andy hope, and he hugged his father longer and tighter than he'd ever hugged him before.

Martin was surprised at the gesture, but finally let the pad and pencil fall to the rain-soaked floor and wrapped his arms about his son. There they stood until Dara called them to dinner.

Martin promised Andy his room would be repaired just as it was before, but Andy knew nothing could ever be just as it was before, not his room, not his town, not his planet. It had all changed because he had changed inside, and saw every familiar sight through different eyes. Even the idea of model spaceships hanging from the ceiling on thin strands of fishing line seemed silly after the real thing had skidded to a halt in his front yard.

Two weeks later, West Bend Middle School reopened under the belief that children in the valley needed structure. Walking through the rainy forest that first day back, Andy declined to play Zoink with Hector and Charlie. As Hector explained the finer points of the game to her, Andy fell behind and sat on a moss-covered log until their voices faded. He felt the cold rain trickle across his face, but it wasn't a wet annoyance anymore. The rain was part of a larger fabric, one thread in a remarkable tapestry. It nourished the plants and trees, the bugs and birds that nested in them, and the animals that fed upon them.

Andy leaned his head back and tugged off his hood. He let the light mist, which was not quite a steady drizzle, fall over his face, then rubbed his hands across his cheeks and through his wet hair. It was long and unruly. He needed a haircut. There was no place for sloppiness anymore, for behind the clouds and the sky, beyond the tug of the earth and the misty atmosphere it held close, a great universe was waiting and watching.

THE END

He felt the cold rain trickle across his face,

but it wasn't a wet annoyance anymore.

ABOUT THE AUTHOR

Writer and filmmaker Dale Kutzera worked as a screenwriter for over ten years. He is a recipient of the Carl Sautter Screenwriting Award, the Environmental Media Award, and participated in the Warner Brother Writers Workshop. He writes about writing and filmmaking at www.DaleKutzera.com.

If you enjoyed *Andy McBean and the War of the Worlds*, please tell your friends and post a review on Amazon.com, Goodreads.com, and any other site you can think of. To learn about the further adventures of Andy McBean, sign up for the newsletter at www.AndyMcBean.com.

H.G. WELLS

H.G. Wells was a prolific writer, penning novels in many genres as well as non-fiction, essays, and even textbooks. A childhood accident resulted in a broken leg, and during the long months of bed-rest, he sought adventure in novels. Making good use of the local library, he became so well-read that he later worked as a teacher and studied biology and political reform. His most famous stories are *The Time Machine, The Invisible Man, The Shape of Things to Come*, and *The War of the Worlds*. Born in 1866, he lived to the age of 80 and saw many of the social and technological advancements he imagined in his stories come true.

Made in the USA
Las Vegas, NV
08 December 2020